what the world will look like
when all the water leaves us

what the world will look like when all the water leaves us

stories by

Laura van den Berg

db
DZANC
BOOKS

DZANC BOOKS

1334 Woodbourne Street
Westland, MI 48186

www.dzancbooks.org

These stories, often in different forms, first appeared in the following publications:

"Where We Must Be," *The Indiana Review* & *The Best American Nonrequired Reading 2008*.
"Goodbye My Loveds," *American Short Fiction*.
"We Are Calling to Offer You a Fabulous Life," *The Northwest Review*.
"Inverness," *Third Coast*.
"The Rain Season," *The Baltimore Review*.
"Up High in the Air," *The Boston Review* & *Best New American Voices 2010*.
"Still Life with Poppies," *The Literary Review*.
"What the World Will Look Like When All the Water Leaves Us," *One Story* & *The Pushcart Prize XXXIV: Best of the Small Presses*.

Published 2009 by Dzanc Books
Book design by Steven Seighman

09 10 11 5 4 3 2 1
First edition October 2009

ISBN-13: 978-0-9767177-7-5

Printed in the United States of America

contents

To my mother, Caroline Merritt,
and to my father, Egerton van den Berg.

where we must be

S ome people dream of being chased by Bigfoot. I found it hard to believe at first, but it's true. I was driving back from Los Angeles in August, after a summer of waiting tables and failed casting calls, when I saw a huge wooden arrow that pointed down a dirt road, "actors wanted" painted across it in white letters. I was in Northern California and still a long way from Washington, but I followed the sign down the road and parked in front of a silver airstream trailer. It was dark inside and I felt the breeze of a fan. The fat man behind the desk said he'd never hired a woman before. And then he went on to describe exactly what happens at the Bigfoot Recreation Park. People come here to have an encounter with Bigfoot. Most of their customers have been wanting this moment for years. I would have to lumber and roar with convincing masculinity. I can do that, I said, no problem. And I proved it in my audition. After putting on the costume and staggering around the trailer for a few minutes, bellowing and shaking my arms, I stopped and removed the Bigfoot mask. The fat man was smiling. He said I would always be paid in cash.

Today I'm going after a woman from Albuquerque. She's small and sharp-shouldered, dressed in khaki shorts and a pink sweatshirt. I'd be willing to bet no one knows she's here. For a brief time, this woman will be living in another world, where all that matters is escaping Bigfoot. People say the park is great for realigning their priorities, for reminding them that survival is an active choice. I'm watching her from behind a dense cluster of bushes. The fat man has informed me that she wants to be ambushed. This isn't surprising. Most people crave the shock.

My breath is warm inside the costume. The rubber has a faintly sweet smell. I like to stroke my arms and listen to the swishing sound of the fake fur. The mask has eyeholes, but blocks my peripheral vision, so I can only see straight ahead. The fat man says this is an unexpected benefit of not having more advanced masks. According to him, Bigfoot is a primitive creature, not wily like extraterrestrials or the Loch Ness Monster, and only responds to what's directly in front of him. Two other people work at the park, Jeffrey and Mack, but our shifts never overlap. The fat man thinks it's important for us to not see our counterparts in person, to believe we are the only Bigfoot.

I wait for the woman to relax, watching for the instant when she begins to think: maybe there won't be a monster after all. I can always tell when this thought arrives. First their posture softens. Then their expression changes from confused to relieved to disappointed. More than anything the ambush is about waiting the customer out. I struggle to stay in character during these quiet moments; it's tempting to consider my own life and worries, but when the time comes to attack, it will only be believable if I've been living with Bigfoot's loneliness and desires for at least an hour.

The woman yawns and rubs her cheek. She bends over and scratches her knee. She stops looking around the forest. Her expectations are changing. She checks her watch. I start counting backwards from ten. When I reach zero, I pound into the clearing and release the first roar: a piercing animal sound still foreign to my ears.

Jimmy and I are sprawled out in his backyard, staring through the branches of a pear tree. Earlier I found him sitting on the front porch, trying to stop a nosebleed. I told him to tilt his head back, then pressed the tissue against his nostrils and watched the white bloom into crimson. It's not love. Or at least not what I thought love would feel like. It hurts to be near him and it hurts to be away.

"What do you dream about?" I ask.

"Of a time when the world was nothing but water."

I spread my legs and arms and imagine floating in an enormous pool. Jimmy lives across the street from the bungalow I've been renting since August, a long structure with low ceilings and chipped turquoise paint. When I first moved into the neighborhood, he dropped by and offered to give me a hand. I didn't really have anything to unpack, but invited him inside anyway. He grew up in Oregon and, after high school, drifted over to California, where he took a job as a postman. He was willowy and pale, with dark hair and green eyes and long eyelashes. He didn't look like anyone else I knew. I pulled a bottle of Jim Beam out of my suitcase and he ended up staying the night.

He rolls toward me, leaving a silhouette of flattened grass. "What about you?"

"I don't remember my dreams," I say. "I can't get them to stay with me."

A hawk with white-tipped wings crosses the sky; I wonder where the bird is headed. It's mid-October. The weather is cool and breezy. "I wish we could keep winter from coming," I tell him.

"Yeah," he says. "It's a real shame."

Jimmy told me he was sick the morning after we met. We were sitting on the floor of my living room, drinking water to ease the hangover. I raised my glass and pointed at the grit pooled in the bottom. He shrugged and said the water has always looked that way. Then he told me about the cold that lasted for three months and the clicking sound of the X-ray machine and the spot on his lungs. When I asked if he had help, he said he'd lost touch with his friends in Oregon and hadn't made any new ones in the postal service. His father was dead, and his mother married a carpet salesman and moved east a few years back. His mother tried to arrange a nurse once his outcome became definite, but he refused, saying he didn't want a stranger in the house. He stopped delivering mail months ago and was collecting disability checks.

He told me all this and then said he'd understand if I minded and we could just go back to being neighbors. But I told him I didn't mind at all. My older sister, Sara, used to have seizures, though I didn't mention that to Jimmy. As a child, I saw her collapse on tennis courts and roller-skating rinks, in the school cafeteria and on the carpeted floor of our bedroom, her chest heaving like something terrible was trying to get out. My mother made her wear a red bicycle helmet whenever she left the house. My mother, who raised us on her own, worked night shifts at a hospice center. Sometimes, out of nowhere, I remember the scent of rubbing alcohol and ointment on her hands.

"How was work?" Jimmy asks.

"Not bad." I stretch my legs and bump against a browning pear. At the end of the summer, the branches were heavy with fruit, but halfway through September, the pears began rotting and falling to the ground. "I gave a woman from Albuquerque a good scare."

"You can practice your roar today if you want," he says. "Since we're already outside."

"I can only do it when I'm in costume." I kick the pear and listen to it roll through the grass. "It's impossible to get into character if I'm not wearing it."

He moves closer and presses his face into my neck. "You would've made a wonderful actress," he mumbles into my skin.

Whenever Jimmy asks about my months in Los Angeles, I tell him how difficult it was to make enough money, how alien I felt carrying trays through a chic bistro that boasted a fifteen-page wine list and thirty-dollar desserts. How I used to dream of fame, of seeing my face staring back at me in magazines and hearing the echo of my voice in dark theaters and never being lonely. When he wants to know about the acting, I tell him the casting directors said I wasn't talented enough. I don't tell him that they often praised my poise and personality, but in the end all said the same thing: you just aren't what we're looking for. I don't tell him this felt worse than having them say I wasn't pretty or gifted because it gave me a dangerous amount of hope.

I touch the back of Jimmy's head. His hair feels damp. In my mind, I list the things I need to help him with over the weekend: wash the sheets, mop the floors, gather all the rotten pears. Just when I think he has gone to sleep, he looks up and asks me to stay with him tonight. I tell him that I will. He lowers his head and we both close our eyes. The late afternoon sun burns against us.

I wake to the boom of a loudspeaker. A truck from the water company is inching down the street. *We are running tests. Do not be alarmed if your water is rusty.* The water has never looked right here. People complain and the company comes out for an inspection, but it never seems to get any better.

Jimmy is still asleep, a spindly arm draped above his head. I don't wake him before I go, even though I know he'd like me to. I want to be alone now, although as soon as I'm on my own, I'll only want to be back with him. I leave a glass of murky water and his pills on the bedside table. He doesn't stir when I kiss the side of his face and whisper a goodbye.

Across the street, I find a letter from my mother in the mailbox. As I open the envelope, a picture of my sister's pepper plants falls to the floor. My sister is married to an architect and lives in Olympia. She hasn't had a seizure in years. She works in a library and has a garden that produces vegetables of extraordinary size: cucumbers big as logs, eggplants that resemble misshapen heads, pepper plants like the ones in the photo, bright green and the size of bananas. In her letter, my mother reminds me that I won't be young forever, that the longer I go without a real job, the more my employability will decrease. I slip the letter and the photograph back into the envelope and tuck it into a chest drawer, which is crowded with other letters she and my sister have sent. When I write back, I end up talking about the arid heat and the blue lupine that grows on the roadside, with only a vague line or two about having found acting work and a house to rent. They know nothing about my Bigfoot costume, about Jimmy.

I undress and take a shower. The water is a cloudy red. The color makes me queasy and I get out before rinsing away all the shampoo. My hair is light without really being blond and the dry climate has made the skin on my knees and elbows rough. I have an hour before work, although I wish I could go in early. I'm starting to realize I can't stand to be anywhere, except stomping through the forest in my Bigfoot costume. That's the reason I always wanted to be an actress: when I'm in character, everything real about my life blacks out.

In the living room, I turn the television to *General Hospital*. I scrutinize the women, golden-skinned and tall, who are playing the minor parts I once auditioned for— the nurse, the secretary, the woman lost in a crowd—then start doing lunges in preparation for my current role. It's essential my muscles stay long and supple, so I can skulk with persuasive simianness.

The phone rings and it's Jimmy. He wants me to come over for breakfast. I tell him I'm late for work, which is about thirty minutes away from being true, and that I have to finish rehearsing.

"I thought you just do stretching exercises." The connection is bad and his voice pops with static.

"It's more complicated than that," I reply. "Any actor will tell you it pays to do your homework."

He relents and makes me promise to come over after work. When I ask what he has planned for today, he says he's going through the jazz records in his closet.

"There's a guy from high school I'd like to mail some of them to."

"Don't you want to talk to him or try to visit?" I ask. "If you've already gone to the trouble of getting his address."

"No," he says. "I really do not."

I walk over to the window and look across the street. Jimmy is standing by his living room window, waving and holding the phone against his ear. He's only wearing his boxers and through the glass, his figure is pale and blurred.

"I was wondering how long it was going to take you," he says.

"Doesn't it feel weird to see the person you're talking to?" I ask. "The whole point of the phone is long distance communication."

"Talking to you isn't the same when I can't see your face," he says. "It's impossible to tell what you're thinking."

"Do I give away that much in person?"

"More than you know." He presses his face against the pane, so his features look even more sallow and distorted.

"Okay," I tell him. "Now I'm really going to be late for work."

After we hang up, we stand at our windows a little longer. His hair is disheveled and sticking up in the back like dark straw. He gives me one last wave, then disappears into the shadows of the house. I wait to see if he'll come back, but the sun shifts and the glare blocks my view. I imagine him watching me from another part of the house, through some secret window. I return his wave to let him know I'm still here.

The fat man says my client wants to kill Bigfoot. The customer is a man from Wisconsin, who came equipped with his own paint ball gun. He tells me not to ambush, but let the man sneak up on me and then moan and collapse after he fires.

"I didn't know killing Bigfoot was part of the deal," I tell him.

The fat man is sitting behind his desk. He leans back in his chair and picks something out of his teeth with the corner of a matchbook. "It's a recreation park," he says. "They get to do whatever they want."

When I first started at the park, my costume had to be specially sized, with lifts in the feet and extra padding sewn into the body. As the fat man took my measurement in the trailer, I asked how people found this place, and he told me about taking out ads in magazines for Bigfoot enthusiasts and about the sightings that had happened in this part of California. Just last fall, his cousin had seen Bigfoot in the woods behind his house, pawing through an abandoned garbage can.

I open the closet and take out my costume. My initials are written on the tag in black marker. "So this guy is going to shoot me with paint balls?"

"To be honest, you might feel a little sting," he says. "But I've banned any other kind of weapon after an old Bigfoot got shot in the face with a pellet gun."

"Ouch."

"It was at close range too. He was covered in welts for days." He runs a hand over his head. "If the weapon doesn't look like a paint ball gun, then shout your safe word."

I step into the costume. "I have a safe word?"

"I don't like to tell people when they first start the job, in case they scare easily."

"I don't." I seal myself inside the rubber skin. "What's my safe word?"

"*Jesus*," he says. "It's really more for the customers, but this is a different kind of situation."

"How'd you come up with *Jesus*?"

"You'd be surprised at how religious some people are," he says. "I always thought screaming *Jesus* would get their attention."

I lower the Bigfoot mask onto my head and inhale the sweet scent of the rubber. Through the eyeholes, I can only see the fat man and his desk.

"And what if this guy doesn't believe in God?"

"Then you've still got the element of surprise."

I've been pretending to not see the man from Wisconsin for over an hour. He's positioned in the branches of a cedar: back pressed against the tree trunk, nose of the paint ball gun angled toward the ground. He's wearing sunglasses and a baseball cap, so I can't see his face or eyes. He paid for two hours and most of our time has passed. He must be saving the killing for the very end.

In the meantime, I've been trying to do the things Bigfoot might actually do. I ambled around, rubbed my back against a tree, ripped up some wildflowers. I sniffed the air and gave two magnificent roars. But the whole time I felt myself slipping out of character and soon I was only a person in the woods, waiting for something painful to happen. I wonder if this is how Jimmy feels when he wakes in the morning—alone and waiting to be hit.

One evening, when it was still summer, we made a picnic and drove to the lake down the road. We ate pears and ham sandwiches and had a long talk about the days when he was first diagnosed and receiving treatment in a hospital a few hours away from our houses and the Bigfoot park. He's young—thirty, only four years older than me—and says he's never even held a cigarette; it wasn't until the hospital that he began to overcome the shock, to look ahead and weigh all that did and did not await him. He would sit around with the other patients and talk about what they would do if the chemotherapy and radiation and surgeries failed, if their hand was called, as he put it. Some wanted to travel to exotic places, while others wanted to find lost lovers or make amends with children they had neglected. Jimmy said he wanted to drive to the Grand Canyon and stay until he was no longer impressed with the view. He couldn't say why he chose that destination, only that it was the first thing that came to him. But he didn't go to the Grand Canyon and he couldn't say why that happened either. It wouldn't have been so hard, he told me, only a long car ride and a little money. After that night, I thought a lot about why he never went out to Arizona and finally decided it was fear—of having the experience fall short, of realizing too late that he should have made a different choice. For him, it was better to not know what the Grand Canyon looked like, to retain the splendor of his dreams.

I'm so caught up in my waiting and thinking and not being Bigfoot that the shots come as a terrible shock. Two red splats in the center of my brown chest. I fall on my back, my furry legs and arms rising and then hitting the ground with a thump. Air rushes from my lungs; I gasp underneath the mask. A rock digs into my back, and there's a sharp pain in my forehead. I hear branches snapping, footsteps. The man is standing over me, still holding the gun. He's shorter than he looked in the tree, with pasty skin and knobby elbows, a white smudge of sunscreen on the tip of his nose. He's wearing a tee-shirt with a bull's eye on the front and camouflage pants.

He nudges me with the toe of his boot and, forgetting I'm supposed to be dead, I squirm to the side. He frowns and raises the gun. I remember my safe word, but I don't say it. I want to believe I stopped myself because I am playing this role to perfection, because I want the killing to be as good as this man hoped, because if he's dying, I want him to walk away feeling satisfied with his life. But the truth is, my chest burns and I'm dizzy and I open my mouth to say *Jesus* and no sound comes out.

He shoots me once in the neck and again in the shoulder. I shriek and press my rubber paw against my arm. I hear quick footsteps, then nothing at all. When my breathing steadies and I'm able to stand, I take off the mask and touch the hard lump on my neck. The ground is speckled with red paint. The man is gone.

"I was always one of those people who assumed I had my whole life to do whatever I wanted," Jimmy says without any prompting. He talks like this all the time now. I call them philosophy spells.

"Like what?" I'm sitting at his kitchen table, drinking a whiskey and coke. Jimmy has yet to comment on the welt on my neck, which has swollen to the size of a lemon. The bumps on my chest are smaller, but still bright pink. I came home late because I had to clean my costume in the trailer's bathroom. I picked off the dead leaves that were stuck to the fur, then placed the suit in the bathtub and rinsed away the red paint with a detachable shower head.

"I don't know," he says. "See the Great Wall of China. Climb a mountain. Get married. Have a kid." He opens a beer and joins me at the table. "The point is I never felt much urgency."

"The last two aren't exactly the kind of thing you'd want to rush into."

"I guess," he replies. "But maybe the only reason we tell ourselves that is because we think we have all this time." He spreads his arms and turns his palms upwards; the skin on his wrists is as translucent as tracing paper. I remember him telling me about his last day of work, how the weight of the bag bruised his shoulder and he carried it until he couldn't anymore, how he dumped all the mail onto the sidewalk and began tearing through the pile: phone bills, postcards, renewal notices, credit card offers, booklets of coupons. He told me that even though he'd never become close with anyone on his route, he was suddenly overcome with a desire to know what their lives contained. Because of his health, he didn't get into much trouble, but was talked into resigning with a year of disability compensation. They only agreed to the disability because they knew the payments would outlive me, he says whenever the checks come, though he lets me take them to the bank and make his deposits all the same.

We're quiet for a while. I finish my drink and make myself another, this time pouring straight whiskey into the glass. The ceiling light flickers. Earlier in the evening, I washed the dishes and scrubbed the floor. The room looks dull and empty. When I offer to get Jimmy a second beer, he shakes his head and squeezes the can until the metal dents. I stand behind him and rest a hand on his shoulder. He lets me do what I know best: acquiesce, accommodate, allow my desires to melt like wax around the emergency of another life.

"It's almost a relief to not consider the future," he says. "To not wonder if I'll find what I was looking for or just be disappointed. Everything falls away in the face of this." He tips his head back and looks at me. His eyes are bloodshot. "So it doesn't really matter if you love me or not, does it?"

"Of course it does," I tell him because I think it's the right thing to say. With Jimmy it seems more important to say the right thing than to be honest. Or maybe I have it backwards. But it does matter in a way, although not in the sense that it could change what's happening to him.

"What did you do at work today?" he asks. I can tell he wants to change the subject.

"I got killed."

"They can do that?"

"Apparently."

"Is that why you've got that lump on your neck?"

"Yep." I brush a clump of hair from his forehead. "Shot dead with a paint ball gun."

He hunches over the table and hangs his head. I prepare myself to comfort. He surprises me with laughter.

At two in the morning, I'm woken by a barking dog. By the time I kick away the covers and sit up, the sound has already faded. My head is fogged with the remnants of a dream, but all I can see is blood on the corner of my sister's mouth drying into a shape that resembles a Rorschach blot. Jimmy is curled underneath the sheets, his breathing nearly imperceptible. I watch until my eyes adjust to the darkness and I can make out the rising and falling of his chest. His face is pressed into the pillow, his lips parted so I can see the wet bulge of his tongue.

I get out of bed and wander into the kitchen. I can still smell the cleaning products I used on the floor. I open the refrigerator and hang my head inside the cool fluorescent glow until the light hurts my eyes. Then I hoist myself onto the kitchen counter, lift the phone to my ear, and dial my sister's number. As the phone rings, I remember the late hour and nearly hang up, but Sara is already mumbling on the other end of the line.

"How's the garden?" I ask. "Grown any squash the size of bowling pins yet?"

"Is everything okay over there?" I imagine her groping the bedside table for her glasses.

"Everything is kind-of-fine. Does that count as an answer?"

"Jean," she says. "I'm going back to bed if you don't tell me what's going on."

What she really wants to know is what I'm still doing in California and what exactly is this acting role I mentioned in a postcard and how much longer before I come back to Washington. I try to think of a way to explain everything, but I can't explain Bigfoot or Jimmy or why the reddish color of the water here makes me think of the fear that swallowed our childhood the way a snake swallows mice. All I know is that I'm in what I'm in and I don't want to leave it, not yet. I hear Sara's breath, deep and impatient, on the line—my sister the survivor, my sister the pragmatist, an overgrown vegetable garden her sole form of excess. I apologize for calling so late, then hang up the phone.

The house seems smaller in the night and I suddenly want to be outside. I go out the back door and sit on the concrete steps. The sky is black and starless. I'm wearing a pair of Jimmy's boxers and one of his T-shirts. Both fit me perfectly. Before we went to bed tonight, he came into the bathroom while I was brushing my teeth. He didn't say anything at first, just stood in the doorway and stared. And then, as I rinsed the spearmint toothpaste from my mouth, he asked if I would like to have some of his clothes. It was the first time he'd mentioned anything about his belongings and I'd been happy to avoid the subject altogether. I spit green into the sink and watched it swirl into the drain. I mean when we're not doing this anymore, he continued. After it's all over. I turned from the sink and told him I'd take whatever he wanted me to have. He didn't say anything else, just nodded and walked into the bedroom.

A rotten pear sits on the bottom step. I reach down and pick it up. This one is really far gone, dark and sticky in my hand like an exposed organ. A kidney, perhaps. Or some kind of decayed heart. I throw the pear and it smacks the trunk of a tree, exploding with a sound like a muffled gunshot. I sit in the stillness of the yard for a moment longer, then wipe my palm on the steps and go inside.

"You don't have to stay here," Jimmy says when I return to bed. "If you're having trouble sleeping."

"I've been sleeping fine," I reply. "Something just woke me."

"I thought I heard you talking to someone."

"I made a phone call." I roll onto my side. "Did I ever tell you about my sister?"

"The one in Olympia, with the mutant vegetable garden?"

"The one and only." I touch the space beneath his collarbone. "Did you know that when we were young, she had these attacks?"

"Attacks?"

"Seizures. She was sick for a long time."

"Did she get better?"

"Yes," I say. "She's fine now."

"What were you doing in the backyard?"

I tell him about finding the pear and the noise it made when it splattered against the tree. I tell him how I've always had good aim, ever since I played in my first softball game as a kid. I flex my arm and he squeezes the small swell of muscle, pretending to be impressed.

"Maybe that's what I'll do tomorrow," he says. "Smash the rest of the pears against the tree." He flattens my hand against his chest. "Pop, pop, pop."

I ask if he finished sorting the records in his closet, which ones he ended up sending to his friend.

"I mailed him my Django Reinhardt's."

"Why did you pick those?"

"Because Django has the most interesting story," he says. "Do you know it?"

I shake my head, my hair rustling against the pillow.

"Django's first wife made paper flowers for a living and one night they caught on fire. It's said Django knocked over a candle, but no one knows for sure. Half his body was badly burned, including his left hand, his guitar hand. His doctors thought he would never play again. But he did. And he became the greatest."

"What does that have to do with your friend?"

"Nothing. I just wanted to share the story with someone. And he lives too far away to drop by for one of those final visits. All the way out in Hawaii, if you can believe it."

A light rain begins to fall. We both turn quiet. I hear the barking dog again. I can't tell which end of the street it's coming from, the noise at once distant and immediate. Soon Jimmy's breathing becomes hushed and I know he's drifted off. I keep my hand on his chest. His bones shift beneath his skin.

When I get to work the next day, the fat man says we need to talk. I stand in front of his desk, my wrists crossed behind my back. The welt on my neck is still large, the color a dark purple. I wonder if he's giving me another customer with a special request.

"Jean," he begins and I realize it's the first time he's ever said my name. I know right away that this isn't about a new assignment. It's always a bad sign when someone who never says your name suddenly starts. "Your last customer wasn't satisfied with his Bigfoot experience."

I tell him how difficult it was to wait for so long, how I kept dipping in and out of character, how I was so used to being the attacker, I couldn't keep the same momentum while pretending to be prey. I promise to work on this angle, to stand in my backyard and imagine I'm being stalked by something awful and wait for it to come.

The fat man shakes his head. "No," he says. "That's not the problem."

"What did the man say?"

"He said you fell like a girl."

I say that's impossible, explaining how I deliberately let my torso hit the ground first, the way Bigfoot would, and refrained from shoving out an arm to lessen the impact. "I know how to fall," I tell him.

"The man said you flailed your arms and squealed. He said the moment you fell, he knew it was a woman in costume, not Bigfoot, and the dream was broken."

I point at the welt on my neck. "He shot me two more times while I was on the ground."

The fat man shrugs. "Maybe he doesn't like women."

I open the closet and push through the other Bigfoot costumes, looking for mine, the smallest one with my initials on the tag. When I don't find it, I slam the door and press my lips together.

"I had to give him a refund." He rises from his chair, lifts my Bigfoot costume from underneath his desk, and hands it to me. "Sorry, Jean."

He's being nice enough to not fire me directly, to let me figure it out for myself, so I don't give him a hard time. I don't yank the other costumes from the hangers. I don't swipe my arm across his desk. I don't strike a match and set the whole place on fire. I take the costume, then open the door and go outside. The sky is a deep, cloudless blue. The winds are high and grey dust rises around me, as though I'm standing in the quiet center of a storm.

I've been walking for twenty minutes and haven't seen a single person on the road. It's two miles from the park to my house. The costume is light in my arms, the fur soft. The wind keeps blowing specks of dirt into my eyes, so I put on the mask. After getting fired, I'm glad to be walking; parts of my body feel so heavy, I worry if I sat down for too long, I'd never get up.

I find myself thinking of things that haven't come into my mind for months. Like how I was married once, to a guy from Tacoma, who I met while working as a receptionist at a local theater company in Washington. We eloped to Las Vegas and were married in a tiny white chapel. It lasted less than a year. I always knew when he was seeing another woman. He had such a terrible game face, it was almost charming. After we split, my sister asked me what I'd expected, marrying someone on a whim. I'd already decided to move to Los Angeles and joked that I did it so I'd be able to channel the pain into my acting. Only it turned out that nobody wanted to see real suffering, that no director or casting agent wanted the kind of pain that would, even for an instant, make anyone want to turn away, like the pain I see when I'm with Jimmy.

It's occurred to me that part of his appeal is the guarantee, as much as anything can be guaranteed, that he will love me and only me for the rest of his life. He will die loving me. By default, of course—he doesn't have the time to find someone else. But if I could grant him more years, enough time to make it likely that he would abandon me for another woman, I would do it. I said this to him one night, when we were in the backyard, underneath the tree, telling the truth for once. Then you do love me after all, he replied, a smile spreading across his hollowed face. And I wondered if he might be right.

A red truck passes on the road, flecking my skin with gravel. I catch the driver staring at me in his side mirror. The wind has settled. The sky is still a clear blue, the brightness of the sun muted by some transparent sheet of cloud. It isn't long before I see the low peak of Jimmy's house in the distance.

"I need to get in the water," he tells me when I turn up at his door, the costume pressed against my chest, the mask still on. His eyes are wild and determined. He doesn't seem to notice that I'm wearing a Bigfoot mask. I worry he's beginning to get delirious, which the doctors told him might happen toward the end.

"You're cracked," I say. "You get tired after picking up a few pears in the backyard."

"I need you to drive me to the lake." He steps onto the porch and closes the door behind him.

"But you could get a cold," I protest, pulling off the mask. A cold for Jimmy could be deadly. "And then you'll be back in the hospital, which is exactly where you don't want to be."

"I had that dream again," he says, glossing over my practical concerns. "Where the world is made of water. I woke up knowing I had to go to the lake today." He looks longingly across the street, at my dented gray car. "And anyway, my body is where I don't want to be, but there's no changing that, is there?"

"I'm low on gas."

He steps off the porch. "There's a station on the way."

"Remember when you told me you never learned to swim?"

"I don't know how to swim," he says. "But you do."

He crosses the street and eases himself into the passenger seat. When I hesitate, he honks the horn. I wonder if he's just trying to make everything go more quickly and has decided to enlist my help. Today it's swimming, tomorrow skydiving. The thought paralyses me. It's an effort for him to sit at the kitchen table or on the porch for a few hours. After we make love, which we're doing less and less, he rolls onto his side and plunges into a deep sleep, as though he's been drugged. I hear the engine start, which means he's found the keys in the cupholder. I consider telling him I've just been fired and don't feel like swimming, but he wouldn't care. And he shouldn't. He honks the horn again. I sprint across the street and join him.

I park underneath a sequoia and toss the keys into the glove compartment. Late afternoon sunlight pours through the windshield, illuminating ridges of dust on the dashboard. We haven't been here since summer and the woods surrounding the lake look darker, more dense. I watch Jimmy get out of the car and walk to the edge of the lake, moving with all the speed he can muster. The Bigfoot costume and mask are heaped in the backseat, hollow and limp. They look like nothing special now, just a pile of rubber and synthetic fur.

I leave the car and stand with Jimmy on the bank of the lake. He removes his shoes and T-shirt, then unbuttons his jeans. He asks me to take off my clothes. The lake is a mile from the main road, shielded by trees and overgrown bushes. I feel emboldened by the enclosure and slip out of my shorts and blouse. I fold our clothes and place them on the knotted roots of a tree, align our shoes so they're side by side. Once he's naked, Jimmy wades into the lake, extending his arms for balance. I wait until his knees disappear beneath the surface, then follow. The water is cold.

"This is too shallow," he says. "Let's go out there." He points to the thick darkness in the center of the lake.

"That will be too deep," I tell him. "You won't be able to stand."

"I don't want to feel anything underneath me." He tucks a loose strand of hair behind my ear. His wet hand slides down my throat and rests against my collarbone. "Will you teach me to float?"

"I'll do my best," I say, meaning it. "But we have to start in shallow water."

He nods. I tell him to let his body go slack. He relaxes a little, but it's not enough. I tell him to let himself sink and when the water rises over his shoulders, I place my hands beneath his back and turn his body horizontal. We manage this in one graceful movement, like synchronized swimmers rehearsing a number.

"The trick is to let your arms and legs dangle, but keep your back firm."

"I can do that," he says.

I take away my hands and after he's floated on his own for a while, I grip his upper arms and swim into the deep. I tell him to close his eyes, to not think about trying to stay above water, to pretend my hands are still pressing against his spine. The muscles in my thighs burn from treading and holding onto Jimmy. His black hair is glossy, his eyelashes long and curved. I can see the teardrop shape of his cheekbones, the green and purple veins in his face. He looks so delicate I almost drag him back to shore, but I know that's simply not possible now. After we reach the center of the lake, I release his arms. His position in the water doesn't change. I drift backwards and tell him to open his eyes.

"The sky is spinning," he says.

I tilt my head back; water swallows the ends of my hair. My skin is numb. I see a huge cloud that resembles a mountain range and recall his wish to visit the Grand Canyon. Perhaps the failure to make that journey explains his persistence today. Maybe he has grown tired of seeing things only in dreams.

"How far out are we?"

"All the way in the center," I say. "But don't look. It'll break your focus." For once, he listens to me.

The sun is dropping, a brilliant orange disc with liquid borders. Jimmy is floating on his back, staring up at the sky. His lips are turning blue, but I don't say anything. I've never seen anyone learn to float so quickly before, but maybe people learn faster when they don't have much time. Time. I've grown to hate that word. I think of it often, how much is wasted, how freeing it would be if we weren't always counting. I look at Jimmy, his skin excruciatingly white against the dark water, and wonder if he's stopped paying attention to time, if he's resigned himself to allowing the days to pass until they don't anymore. I think of what he said back at the house, about how his body is where he doesn't want to be, how neither of us are where we want to be, yet somehow, at this moment, we are.

"Will you roar for me?" he asks.

I shift in the water, creating small ripples that push his body farther away.

"Your Bigfoot roar," he continues. "I want to hear an echo."

"I can't."

"Why not?"

"I was fired today." I touch the bump on my neck.

He's quiet for a minute. He doesn't move in the water and I'm proud of him for maintaining his concentration. "That doesn't matter," he finally says. "You can still be Bigfoot."

"It's not as convincing without the costume. I've told you this before."

"Then imagine it," he says. "You're supposed to be an actress, right?"

I shut my eyes and picture Bigfoot lumbering through the forest, more alone than any human could grasp. I imagine the weight of his solitude. I open my mouth and fill my lungs with air, then arch my back and push it all out. The noise that comes from my body is unlike anything I've ever heard before. It beats against the thinning branches and the fall air, shoots towards the clouds like smoke. The echoes last for a long time, the vibrations moving across my skin like electrical currents. When I open my eyes, the lake and treetops are washed in a blue darkness.

Jimmy has floated out of my reach, but I don't swim after him. When the crescent moon turns luminous, he asks to be taken back to the car. I guide him to shore and once he's on dry land, he crouches and begins to shiver violently. I scold myself for not bringing a blanket or towels and try to get him to at least put on his clothes. But he shakes his head and asks me to help him wait it out. It will pass, he tells me. I'm being tested, I realize, to see how long I can endure suffering in another person. I bend over and press my hand between his shoulder blades, feeling the slender ligaments and bones a healthy body conceals. The moonlight makes the lake glow like an enormous black pearl. The soft skin on my stomach hardens with goosebumps. The night is quiet, save for the sound of Jimmy's rapid breath. I kneel next to him, the damp leaves sticking to my knees. I look down at Jimmy's thigh, at the dirt smudged across the pale stretch of skin; I brush it away, the grit damp and cool. I bring my hand to my lips and let the dirt melt off my fingertips, tasting bitterness and metal. The moon shifts and the grass ahead catches silver, the light passing over us and away.

goodbye my loveds

My brother entered my room at dawn. He wanted to show me the hole outside our building. I got out of bed and he drug me through the blue-black light of our basement apartment. He was twelve, although most people thought he was younger. I didn't tell him I was already awake, lying on my back and gazing at the ceiling, trying hard to return to sleep until my alarm sounded, trying hard to be normal.

The streets were quiet, the slender trees dusted in a papery fog. It was warm and humid, the beginning of summer. Denver crouched behind a car. He was wearing swimming trunks and a Superman cape. "Look at that." He pointed to a dark circle on the asphalt. It was the size of a dinner plate, the borders uneven and jagged. "I found it when I was patrolling."

The patrolling started shortly after the school year ended. Denver walked the sidewalks in the early hours to make sure there was no spilled garbage and all the cars were where they should be, no loose pets or broken windows.

"That's just a crack," I told him. "It happens."

"No, Shelby. It's a hole." And to prove it, he reached inside, his arm disappearing to the elbow.

"Okay," I said, hoping he would stop before a rat found the soft tips of his fingers. "You're right. It's a hole."

He pulled out his arm and rocked back on his heels, satisfied.

It looked like a patch of asphalt just melted away, a miniature sinkhole precariously close to the rear of a brown Honda. I knelt on the concrete and peered into the opening. I saw a narrow stream of darkness, as though

I was gazing through a telescope trained on a black and starless sky.

Denver produced a large flashlight from underneath his cape. He pressed a button and for a moment his face was washed in an eerie whiteness.

"You shouldn't be playing with that," I said. "It's for emergencies."

"What kind of emergencies?"

"I don't know," I told him. "Snowstorms, blackouts. That sort of thing."

"But I see emergencies all the time." He cradled the flashlight protectively. "So doesn't it make more sense to keep it with me?"

His hazel eyes widened and his mouth tightened. He was starting to get anxious, which meant this was not the time to force adult logic. "Okay, Denver. That's a good point."

He aimed the light into the hole; the beam was swallowed by shadows. "There's no bottom," he said without looking up.

"Of course there's a bottom," I replied. "We just can't see it."

"It's weird to have a hole without a bottom," he continued, ignoring me as he always did when I contradicted his imaginings. "Maybe it's some kind of tunnel."

A terrible image came into my mind: Denver slipping underneath the street and getting stuck in some dark, underground compartment of the city. I examined the diameter and, to my relief, decided it wasn't large enough for him to squeeze through.

"Come on." I felt the heat of the sun, which had risen above the rows of brick buildings. "Let's go inside. I have to go to work." Soon the neighbors would be out and I didn't want them to see Denver like this, dressed in swimming trunks and a cape, shining his flashlight into a hole. They already thought we were a strange pair, brother and sister living alone together. We'd been on our own for just over a year.

I told my brother it was time to put on some regular clothes.

"I'd rather not," he said.

"Please, Denver." I rubbed my forehead. "I'm tired."

He hesitated for a moment, then clicked off the light and followed me to the apartment. He thanked me for looking at the hole and apologized for waking me so early. I told him it was okay, I was glad to see it. We closed the door just before a car passed on the street.

Our parents were killed in the Amazon. Their guide, Lugo, sent me a letter after the bodies were brought back to the States. It was tradition, he told me, to tell the oldest child the story of their parents' death. In the opening paragraph, he mentioned spending time in Cape Town and learning to speak and write in English. He described the libraries he frequented while abroad and getting hooked on English novelists and, after returning to South America, squeezing copies of *Jude the Obscure* and *The French Lieutenant's Woman* into the backpack he carried on expeditions. He lived in a floating house along the banks of the Amazon River. I could tell from the tone of the letter that he was fond of my parents.

My parents were scientific explorers. They specialized in terrestrial primates and had discovered several new species: a long-tailed monkey in East Africa, a macaque in India, a highland mangabey in Tanzania. Their expeditions were featured in *National Geographic* and *Time Magazine*. They co-authored six books and delivered lectures at Ivy League universities. My brother and I spent most of our childhoods in boarding schools—his in New Hampshire, mine in western Massachusetts—but sometimes the spring and winter breaks coincided with lecture circuits and they'd take us along. I remembered sitting in the front row of auditoriums, Denver's legs barely long enough to reach the floor, and hearing the thunderous applause when they appeared on stage. After they died, my mother's sister came into their house, a pale blue Victorian in Lowell, and started throwing away all the articles and photographs. This is what got them killed, she shouted when I objected, waving a picture of my mother standing with a crocodile at the Great Barrier Reef. Aunt Lucille had been angry because she thought she was going to have to take Denver. The day he heard about our parents, he defaced a statue of the school's founder with black spray paint, and Aunt Lucille received a call from the headmaster, who suggested boarding school wasn't the best place for him right now. I was three semesters away from finishing an art history degree at a college in the Berkshires, but insisted my brother live with me. I left school and took Denver to Boston, where jobs were easy to find and nothing was familiar.

My parents had gone to the Amazon in search of the mapinguary, a giant primate that was nicknamed the Sasquatch of Brazil. In his letter, Lugo talked about floating away from the jungle city of Iquitos, the muddy water, tarantulas, bats, and tree frogs. The shade of the massive canopy leaves. The isula ants—so toxic, a single bite could cause hallucinations—that coated the low-hanging vines. The heads of alligators that, from a distance, resembled floating wood. My mother was skilled at imitating animal calls, particularly birds and monkeys. She had a special empathy for the howler monkeys, he wrote. He said the dangers were too numerous to list and my parents had fallen prey to the greatest: beauty. The Amazonian coral snake was one of the most stunning in the world, black as coal and vividly banded with red and yellow. My parents and Lugo were on land, following a set of unusual tracks, when the coral snake slunk into their path. My mother leaned down to take a picture and the snake leapt forward and bit her wrist. As my father rushed to her side, the snake lunged at his ankle. There was nothing to be done. Not even the river people had developed a remedy for this kind of snakebite. They were both dead within an hour. In my mother's last minutes, she shouted a man's name over and over. Calvin, Lugo said. She kept screaming for Calvin. And it was the most tortured sound he'd ever heard.

I'd looked up from the letter then. I had no idea who Calvin was. In fact, I was positive I had never heard her utter the name before. Perhaps it was a blessing your father died first, Lugo wrote next. And then he signed his name. He listed an address where I could reach him if I wanted to know more. I wrote back right away, filling page after page with questions. I needed to gather the details, to be able to picture the entire story, but Lugo never replied. I'd always intended to let my brother read Lugo's letter—after we moved, after he was settled at his new school, after he stopped waking me in the middle of the night to listen to the noises in the wall. But none of that passed, and I knew he might never hear the whole story. I didn't think it was right, but it was how it had to be.

I worked at a bookstore downtown, a thirty minute T ride from our apartment on the outskirts of Cambridge. The shop specialized in antique books and we averaged about five customers a week, but combined with my parents' estate, doled out in small monthly payments by Aunt Lucille, the salary was enough. The owner had said other employees developed mold allergies and subsequently quit, but I was determined to stick it out and never left home without a bottle of Afrin tucked inside my purse. The bookstore reminded me of my first year in boarding school, the year I ate my lunch in the library while reading *The Count of Monte Cristo* or *Wuthering Heights*, the year books taught me to not be lonely.

Work became harder once it was summer and Denver was out of school. He was attending a day camp at the Cambridge YMCA, where he played tennis and swam, but after finding the hole, he refused to leave the apartment. *They* wouldn't have made me go to camp, he'd said. *They* wouldn't have liked me hanging around with philistines when I could be exploring instead. He was referring to our parents—he had stopped calling them Mom and Dad when we moved to the city—and I was pretty sure "philistine" was a word he'd picked up from our mother (she often used it in reference to Aunt Lucille) and that he didn't even know what it meant, but I was too tired to request a definition. We finally agreed on some guidelines—no going outside the neighborhood, no games involving superglue or fire, no bothering the people next door—but I felt uneasy leaving him alone. He was only twelve and I never knew when he would invent an urgent reason to break one or all of my rules. Still, coming into work had its perks. The Public Gardens were across the street and some afternoons I saw squirrels chasing each other up sycamores, picnickers spreading their blankets across the grass. And this guy dropped by every Wednesday, looking for a first edition of *Moby Dick*.

Jordan was older than me by five years. He always wore jeans, a black T-shirt, and leather sandals. He was clean-shaven and smelled faintly of citrus. We talked whenever he visited and I liked to think that was why he kept coming back, seeing as we'd never had a first edition of *Moby Dick* and had no hope of acquiring one anytime soon. Jordan knew my parents were gone and that I was looking after my brother. I'd told him it was a car crash—my standard line because it didn't lead to more questions.

I hadn't spent much time with anyone but Denver since we came to the city. My last encounter was right after the funeral, with an ex-boyfriend from high school. It happened in the attic of my parents' house, while the wake was bustling downstairs. When it was over, I cried for hours and after trying to console me for a while, he put on his clothes and left. Sex and dating just weren't practical now, with my job and Denver and the violent sadness I was trying to keep from breaking through. And yet today passed slowly because tomorrow was Wednesday and that meant I would see Jordan.

I spent most of the afternoon in the back of the store, the office door cracked so I could hear the bells that jingled whenever someone entered. A Gorky print hung on the wall behind the desk; it was a painting of the artist and his mother, billowy figures done in whites and tans with a single jolt of maroon, the faces round and smudged. I liked to pretend they watched over me while I worked at the computer, which I'd been using to research all the universities where my mother ever lectured or taught, looking for someone named Calvin. During the spring, I exhausted all the places she and my father visited after they became successful, plus Syracuse and Brown, where she'd been an adjunct professor before she married. But this morning on the T, I remembered one place I hadn't checked: a university in Michigan that gave my mother a fellowship after she finished her graduate work. She had talked a lot about winter in Michigan, the pointed icicles that hung from tree branches and the blue gloss of frozen lakes. She had an office on the top floor of a stone building, where she researched her first important paper. It was during that winter in Michigan when she realized she didn't want to be a laboratory scientist, but an explorer, a time before she met my father, a time when she was still discovering who she wanted to be—or had decided to become someone else. I was hopeful as I scanned the roster of current and former faculty, but didn't find what I was looking for. I went through the entire list a second time to be certain. No Calvins.

I leaned back in the chair and looked through the doorway. The air was warm and thick with dust. There was an air conditioner, but it rattled and sputtered, so I kept it off. One section of the store consisted entirely of antique maps. I liked to find maps of the places my parents had been and study the geography, imagining them crossing the blue lines of the Kalambo River in Tanzania or climbing the brown peaks of Mount Abu in India. The phone rang. I ignored it at first, then realized it might be my brother and answered. It was Denver, calling to tell me the hole in the street was actually a tunnel that led to the other side of the world.

Denver greeted me on the sidewalk outside our building. He was dressed normally—corduroy pants and a striped polo shirt—and holding a bright blue yo-yo. A pair of swimming goggles hung from his neck. He told me about the tests he had performed, how he lowered the yo-yo all the way into the hole and still didn't find the bottom, how he put on his goggles and stuck his head underneath the street and saw an endless channel of black.

"That's when I realized it was a tunnel," he said.

He had that steely look, standing with his legs parted, squeezing the yo-yo so hard his knuckles whitened—the same expression he had when the school counselor asked me to pick him up one afternoon in April and on the way home, Denver explained that, while watching a war movie in history class, he had become so convinced the soldiers were going to march through the screen and overtake the school, he ran into the hall and hid in the girls' bathroom so he'd have a chance to escape. When I went to see the guidance counselor the next day, an elfish man with a gray beard and pointed ears, he talked about generalized anxiety and object-related fixations and I imagined paintings from the abstract art class I took in my freshman year, the swirls of color that spiraled together and apart.

I leaned over the hole. "Can I see?"

He handed me his goggles. "Go ahead."

I put on the goggles and kneeled on the sidewalk, trying not to care who might be watching. When I ducked underneath the street, the darkness was cool against my lips and forehead. I caught the faint odor of gasoline, saw a quick movement. Just a shadow, perhaps. Or a rat.

"What do you think?"

"It could be a tunnel." I stood and removed the goggles. "But I doubt it goes to the other side of the world."

He pulled the goggles from my hand and looped them around his neck "Where do you think it goes then?"

I tilted my head to the side, pretending to consider his question. "New Jersey. I bet it goes to New Jersey. Maybe even Rhode Island."

"Don't tell me that," he said. "Don't talk to me like I don't know what I'm doing."

When I suggested he spend more time with neighborhood kids and take a break from the hole, he stormed into the apartment. He should be thinking about girls and sneaking his first beer, but that's not my brother—or at least not the boy that emerged from Aunt Lucille's phone call to the boarding school and the two-coffin funeral. She was the one who drove up to New Hampshire and collected him, while I took the train into Lowell. They were waiting outside my parents' house when the taxi dropped me off,

Aunt Lucille standing on the edge of the driveway, her posture rigid and square, Denver sitting on the front lawn, pulling up fistfuls of grass, the gray house looming behind him. Since then, he'd come to believe in magic, in making the unknowable knowable. I viewed him with equal doses of fear and admiration.

Inside I found him sulking on the pullout sofa in the living room, his makeshift sleeping quarters while we saved for a larger apartment. He had lined the shelves of our bookcase with toy dinosaurs and science books, taped a pink and yellow map of South America to the wall. The last book he read was about scientists digging to the center of the earth to study the rocks and molten core, but it seemed he'd settled for reaching the other side of the world.

Denver told me that he was going to the community pool to swim laps, which I knew was a lie. I didn't know where he really planned to go, only that he wanted to be away from me. When the front door closed, something deep in my body ached.

After my brother had been gone for a while, I found a message from a neighbor on the answering machine, complaining that Denver had spent the day running up and down the sidewalk in his Superman cape, shouting about emergencies. I worried someone might call Children's Services and that Denver would have to go live with Aunt Lucille. I called the neighbor back and told her I had talked things over with Denver and he had promised to not be such a nuisance.

"And the costumes," she pressed. I'd seen this woman around, in her running pants and sweatshirts and pink hair rollers. She smoked skinny cigarettes and owned a black Pomeranian. "What are you doing about the costumes?"

"You mean the Superman cape?"

"It's not normal for a boy his age."

"Listen." I leaned against the kitchen counter, the speckled Formica edge digging into the small of my back. "We've had a hard year, Denver and me."

"You're not the first person life has been unkind to."

I wanted to tell her that she was right in saying we weren't the first to suffer, but sometimes it felt like we were the only people out there with losses so raw and gaping, and that we could both use a little understanding. I didn't say any of this. I thanked her for her time and offered another apology. She reminded me the recycling was supposed to go out on Wednesday, not Tuesday, and then hung up the phone.

My parents weren't getting along the year they died. I was away at college, studying to become an art historian, and never knew all the details. But I could tell when I came home for Thanksgiving and Christmas and spring break that things were not as they always had been. From eavesdropping on late-night arguments, I was able to determine my mother had gotten the credit for discovering the highland mangabey in Tanzania and had been approached by several prominent scientists planning an expedition to Indonesia. My father had not been invited.

It was his idea to look for the mapinguary in the Amazon. My mother had argued it wasn't the best use of their time and research grants, that the creature probably didn't even exist. But in the end, my father convinced her. I could imagine his thoughts as he retreated to his study at the end of their spats and slammed the door: returning from the Amazon victorious, giving interviews to top magazines and talking about how my mother hadn't even believed in the mapinguary and without his intuition and savvy, they never would have located this remarkable specimen.

I took out Lugo's letter and sat on the edge of my bed. I re-read the part about the snake and my mother crying out for Calvin. Sometimes I wondered if he wasn't just trying to ease our grief by giving us an interesting story, a history to carry. Surely my mother, with all her knowledge and experience, would have known better than to get so close to a deadly snake, and I recalled reading that poisonous snakes only struck once before retreating. But perhaps they had gotten too casual and confident after so many years of successful travel. Perhaps this coral snake, for the first and last time in its life, possessed the power to bite twice. It was a place where people lived in floating houses, amongst giant spiders and toxic dart frogs and carnivorous plants. A land of treachery and mystery. I would never know if Lugo's story was what actually happened. If my parents died from the coral snake or yellow fever or something else. If my mother called for Calvin. If my father went first. If they reached for each other at the end. How long it took them to die.

At dusk, Denver came home with two skinned knees, though he wouldn't say how he earned them. He refused my offers to make macaroni and cheese or read aloud from science books, and fell asleep earlier than usual in the living room. I sat on my bed, holding Lugo's letter, until the apartment was dark except for the orange glow of my desk lamp. Denver's body was so quiet that I checked the rhythm of his breath as I slipped outside, where I stood on the sidewalk and stared at the hole. The streetlights gave the perimeter a pale gleam and in the darkness, it seemed deeper, more magnetic. I kneeled and rested my hands over the hole, feeling the heat rise from it like breath. I called into it, softly, and there were no echoes.

The next day, Jordan appeared in the bookstore at his usual time, just after twelve. I was finishing lunch: a cheese sandwich and a can of iced tea. When I heard the bells, I brushed the Wonderbread crumbs from my shirt and dabbed the sides of my mouth with my thumb, then walked out of the office. I had dressed up a little, a white blouse and a loose black skirt, silver bracelets on my wrists.

He was standing at one of the bookcases, examining the spines. The same floppy dark hair and easy posture, a hand in the back pocket of his jeans. He faced me and smiled broadly, his teeth straight and white.

"Any luck?"

"Nope," I replied. "Still haven't been able to get a copy."

"That's too bad," he said. "I had a good feeling about this week."

"You must be an optimist."

He shrugged. "I guess so."

I told him I had some business cards in the office, stores in New York that specialize in rare books and might have what he needs. "I'm guessing you'd be willing to travel for it."

"Sure," he said, still smiling. "Maybe I could even get you to come with me."

"Maybe." When I stepped into the office, heat moved across my cheeks and down my neck. This was the first time we'd ever left the open area of the store. I sat in the chair and rifled through the desk drawer, pushing past paperclips and pencils to look for the business cards. Jordan leaned against the desk and crossed his arms.

"So what's with *Moby Dick*?" I peered into the back of the drawer. "Some kind of phallic obsession?"

When he didn't answer, I looked up from the mess of cards and papers. His lips were bent into a frown.

"Joking," I said.

"I know." His expression softened. "It's just that the book belonged to my wife."

"Wife?"

"Well, she's not my wife anymore," he said. "But she had the copy of *Moby Dick*. A first American edition with green linen binding. It belonged to her grandmother and her mother. She kept it in the drawer of her bedside table, where some people might keep a Bible. One of her favorite things."

"What happened to it?"

He took a pack of Camels out of his pocket. "Mind if I smoke?"

I shook my head. He lit a cigarette, took a drag, then exhaled through his nose. "After she served me with divorce papers, I took the book to a pawn shop and told the man behind the counter to sell it for whatever he could get. Or give it away. I really didn't care. I just never wanted to see it again."

I accidentally squeezed a card for a bookstore in Chicago, the sharp corner pricking my skin. "She must have been upset."

"Devastated. Totally broken up." He stared at the end of his cigarette for a moment. "Got an ashtray?"

I took the empty ice tea can out of the trash and placed it on the desk.

Jordan ashed into the small opening. "So a few months after we split, she's driving with her new boyfriend. They were going to the airport and had to pass through this long tunnel. You know which one I mean?"

"I think so."

"He was speeding. I imagine they might have been arguing. Of course, no one knows exactly how it happened. Just that they crashed in the tunnel and the man died on the spot and my wife a week later, in a hospital. And ever since, I haven't been able to think of anything but that first edition of *Moby Dick*." He dropped the cigarette into the can and it made a hissing noise. "Your parents died in a car accident too, right?"

I resumed looking for the business cards. "Sort of."

"Let me guess. The crash came first and then they were in some kind of vegetative state for a while, right? In a coma, like my wife was?" He whistled. "That must have been tough on you and your brother."

"Yeah," I told him. "It was pretty awful."

I found three cards for New York stores and handed them to Jordan. They had strange and elegant names, like Gotham and Hagstrom. He thanked me and slipped them into his cigarette pack. I tipped back in my chair and stretched, raising one arm over my head.

"Whose work is that?" He pointed at the wall behind me.

"Gorky." I'd asked my boss about the print once and he said it had come with the shop.

He walked over to the picture. "He had a funny first name." He touched the edge of the frame. "Archie, was it?"

"Arshile." I watched him from behind. I did not go to him. "He killed himself, you know. A hanging. His wife left him, his studio burned down, and then he was in an accident that paralyzed his painting arm."

"I remember hearing that story. He left some kind of weird suicide note."

"He wrote it in chalk, on the crate he used to reach the rope." In college, the art students loved to talk about famous artist suicide stories. Malaval's gun and Rothko's knife and Gorky's rope. "'Goodbye my Loveds.' That's what he said."

Jordan came over to the chair. He kneeled at my feet and rested his chin on my leg. My fingers disappeared into his black hair. I leaned in close and asked him to shut the door, my lips grazing his cheekbone. He closed the door, then resumed kneeling in front of me. His hands began at my ankles and glided up my calves and thighs, coming to rest on my hips. My body turned feverish. I had not felt this kind of exhilaration in so long, the subtle thrill of being overtaken coupled with a complete possession of self, when the giving in was both deliberate and desired. I wanted to tell him the truth about my life, but he gently squeezed the sides of my waist, as though he was sculpting my body, and I stayed quiet. I was reaching for the collar of his shirt when I heard the phone. Five rings passed before I answered.

I touched Jordan's chest, then brought the phone to my ear. The voice was unfamiliar and I had trouble making sense of the words. The police. Calling to tell me they had Denver at the station. I told them I would be right there and dropped the phone.

"Let it go, whatever it is." Jordan's hands were still up my skirt. "Stay a little longer."

"I have to leave." When he didn't move, I nudged his leg with the toe of my shoe. "Now. I have to go now."

"Someone in trouble?"

"My brother." I gathered my purse and the keys to the store. I bumped against a stack of magazines and they flew off the desk. I left them scattered across the carpet.

When we stepped outside, I smoothed my hair and straightened my blouse. The sidewalk was crowded, the street clogged with cars. It was hotter than it had been in the morning and my thighs were sticking together. He stood with me while I locked the door, shadowed by the purple awning. I told myself to keep moving, to stop thinking about how I wanted Jordan to continue, about how a part of me wished I could leave Denver in that police station until he snapped out of it and started acting like a normal kid. I was about to walk away when I turned and told Jordan there was something he should know.

"My parents didn't die in a car accident like your wife." I dropped the store keys into my purse and zipped the bag.

"They died in a jungle. I'm sorry for the lie. I won't ever know what really happened to them, so we still have that in common."

He didn't reply right away. He slipped his hands into his pockets and looked at something in the background. His eyes narrowed; his mouth and jawline hardened. "The first time I saw you, I thought you looked like a mess," he finally said.

A group of students brushed past us, carrying backpacks and bottled sodas. I stepped out of their way, trying to decide if this was the moment to say everything or to just let it go. I thought of Lugo's letter arriving from South America, the green stamp in the right corner of the envelope, the musky scent of the paper. I wondered what would have happened if I'd shown Jordan the letter, if he would've believed the story. After a few seconds, I wished him luck with *Moby Dick* because if I said anything about myself, about Denver or Lugo or my parents, I felt like I would start talking and wouldn't be able to stop. Jordan sighed and walked away. I watched until he disappeared into the swarm of bodies. I knew he wouldn't be back next week. For an instant, I forgot all about Denver. When I remembered, I began to run.

The last time I saw my parents was over a year ago, during my spring vacation. They had rented a little house in Wellfleet, a white one-story with navy blue shutters. The interior smelled of seawater and on windy nights a humming sound rose from the tiny holes in the wood planks. On Saturdays we had lobster and corn on the cob, and some evenings my father played *Moonlight Sonata* on the piano while the rest of us sat on the sofa and listened. When I wanted to remember my father as being graceful and kind, I imagined his hands moving over the piano keys like pale stones skipping across a lake. Everyone loved the house except Denver, who had always been frightened of the sea. But even he was content to sit in the dry sand and arrange silver-grey oyster shells in large and intricate patterns, as though he was signaling a rescue plane.

This wasn't long after the expedition in Tanzania and my mother had recently published several articles in major academic journals. My father spent most of the daylight hours locked in the spare bedroom, working feverishly on a paper of his own. He would emerge from his office around five o'clock, eyes bloodshot from staring at the computer screen, his skin sallow and droopy. You should get more sun, my mother would say, walking over and placing a hand on his shoulder. He would shrug away her touch and ask Denver if he wanted to play Frisbee on the beach.

One evening, while my father was grilling sausages and Denver was working on his shell patterns and I was setting the table, my mother came into the kitchen and asked me to walk with her on the beach. She was wearing denim shorts and a sleeveless blouse, her hair pulled into a loose ponytail, her feet bare. I nodded and stepped outside, leaving a heap of silverware and paper napkins on the red tablecloth. We chatted for a while about my courses in Renaissance architecture and Middle Eastern woodcarvings and my roommate, who was majoring in discrete mathematics and always leaving formula-covered sticky notes on the bathroom mirror. The house was a white speck in the distance when my mother stopped and said she wanted to tell me a story.

She and my father had traveled with a small group of scientists in central Vietnam, through the province of Quang Nam. They trekked across valleys and green hills, toward the tropical forests, where they studied the endangered Crested Argus. It kind of looks like a peacock, she told me, only lower to the ground, with violet feathers that grow so long they leave drag marks in the soil.

"But the story isn't about the bird," she said, pushing her toes into the wet sand. "The story I want to tell happened before we even got to the forest, when we camped at the bottom of a hill, near a temple called My Son."

My Son, an L-shaped structure with towers and tunnels, was built in the twelfth century, during the reign of the Champas. She had read a little about the Champas and knew some of the temple's history. The fire that damaged a wall during the sixteenth century and the bombs that toppled one side during the Vietnam War and the symbolism of the towers. They all had three levels: the lowest represented the human world, the middle was for spirits, the top for all things close to humans and spirits.

She hiked up the hill early one morning to see the temple. It was not yet dawn. The rest of the party was still asleep in the tents. There were no villages on the surrounding hills and the rises looked perfectly smooth and dark. She entered My Son and walked down a long tunnel until the path stopped and she saw, through the shadows, an enormous stone face with round eyes and fangs that resembled spears. Sort of like a gargoyle, she said. But different. More frightening. She reached out and touched the mouth. Green moss had grown between the teeth. The stone was cold and rough. She smelled the earth in a way she never had before.

When she came outside, the sun was rising between two hills. She saw a figure walking toward her. The silhouette was dark and wavy, the face obscured. For a moment, she believed it was a stranger coming to tell her something, to show her a secret part of the land. But as the person drew closer, she knew from the height and shape of the head that it was her husband. And that was when she felt it: the flutter in her chest and the voice inside her, unmistakable as the whiteness of the morning sky, telling her to run.

"I almost did," she said. "I almost turned and ran down the hill, through the valley and into the jungle. I can't say what stopped me. Common sense, I suppose, although I've come to believe that's an overrated quality." She bent over and reached into the water. When she stood, a red starfish with two missing tentacles was cupped in her palm. "It's dead. See how the color has lightened?" She pointed to a spot that had faded to pink, then tossed the starfish back into the sea and continued with her story.

"The rest of the trip passed without incident. We went to the tropical forest and studied the Crested Argus. We went home and wrote our papers. And a few weeks later, I found out I was pregnant with you." She rested a hand on her stomach. "But I never forgot that moment by the temple and the voice inside me. In fact, I've been thinking about it a lot lately." She touched my chin with the tip of her finger. "You're getting older, Shelby. And one day, you're going to have such a moment."

The sky was colorless, our dusk-washed conversation turning more surreal by the minute. My mother had never talked like this before. I had always known her as a pragmatist.

"How do you know?" I asked.

"You will. It's a fact of life. Just believe me. And when you do, I want you to run. Even if you're in a forest or in the middle of the ocean. Even if you don't know where you'll spend your next night." She squeezed my elbow. "Do you understand, Shelby?"

"Yes," I said, even though I did not. The beach was dark by the time we turned from the water and linked arms and walked back to the house with blue shutters and gaps in the wall, invisible to the unassisted eye.

A woman from Children's Services met me at the police station. She was dressed in a navy pantsuit that had the sheen of polyester, her gray hair twisted into a bun. When I asked how she got involved, she said a neighbor had called the police and they had called Children's Services. Your brother is a case now, she told me. She said we had to find a place to talk and led me to a bench in a hallway. After we sat down, she took a legal pad and a pen out of her briefcase. I was still thinking about Jordan, the closing of my own little rabbit hole, when the caseworker asked if I understood what would happen next.

"Not really."

"I ask questions and you answer them."

"What exactly did my brother do?"

"He assaulted two city workers repairing a hole in the street. Hit them in the legs with a flashlight. One of them will have to see a doctor. When the police arrived, your brother was very upset about losing his tunnel. Does this make any sense to you?"

"Kind of."

"He was wearing a red cape and swimming goggles when he came into the station. Does he always roam the neighborhood in costume?" She pushed the dark tip of the pen against the paper.

"Not always." I was trying to be as truthful as I could without making the situation worse. "But sometimes."

"We can discuss the incident later," she said. "First I need to get a family history." She looked up at me. One of her blue-gray eyes was cloudy. "The only relative you're in touch with is an Aunt Lucille?"

"That's right."

"What happened to your parents?"

"It's a little complicated," I said.

"Car crash? Sudden illness?"

"You wouldn't believe me if I told you."

"Oh." She lowered her voice. "Was it a murder-suicide? A double suicide?" She reached across the bench and patted my hand. "It's okay, dear. We see that kind of thing all the time."

"No." I rubbed the back of my neck. I was so tired of people getting the story wrong. "That's not it at all."

"What then?"

"You really want to hear the whole thing?"

"I have to." She tapped her pen against the legal pad. "For your brother's file."

I started from the beginning. I told her about our parents' expeditions and the packed lecture halls and the glossy photographs in *National Geographic*. About the floating villages and the howler monkeys and the snake coiled in the grass. Lugo's letter and how I was thinking of writing him again to say *please answer me* or *don't tell me anymore* or *give me the truth this time*. And Calvin. I told her about Calvin and how I had been looking for him, peering into the eyes of strange men, imagining a part of my mother living inside them. I told her about the bookstore and Jordan and his dead wife's first edition of *Moby Dick* and what it was like to feel his hands on my legs. I told her how I had even messed that up, how my life had messed it up, how it seemed like there was no room for anything except staying above the tide. I went on about everything that made sense and everything that didn't. When I finished, I felt like I had been talking for hours.

"That's quite a story," she said, her fingers loosely holding the pen.

"Yes," I told her. "Yes, it is."

"Would you like to see your brother now?" She stood and tucked the legal pad underneath her arm.

I couldn't tell if she was being kind or if she thought I was out of my mind too. I pressed my fingertips against my eyelids. It was becoming clear that none of this was going to be taken care of easily—more than an apologetic call to a neighbor or chat with the school guidance counselor. I followed her down a long hallway. The clicking of her shoes reminded me of crickets in July.

Denver was sitting in a dark and windowless room, resting his arms and head against the table. His cape and goggles were missing. The largeness of the space made him look small and pale. As I stood by the closed door and felt the weight of his stare, I remembered the instant in which I realized my brother was going to live with me. That I was going to leave school, my thick art history texts and numerically gifted roommate, and might not ever return to any of it. That I understood everything my mother had said on the beach. That I was having my moment.

Aunt Lucille was driving us back to the house after the funeral, my brother and me in the backseat. He kept tugging at the tight knot of his black tie, and my mind emptied as I gazed into his eyes, finding nothing but sadness and wants. The voice came as we passed a park, empty save for a gray pack of pigeons, but instead of leaving, I tracked down an old boyfriend and pulled him into the attic and then wept for days. My brother would hug my knees and tell me not to cry and I would feel ashamed for even thinking of leaving him. It still came on every now and then, when I watched Denver toss in his sleep or stare too long at his map of South America—nothing more than a shudder of strange, liquid energy, but sometimes I had to stand outside the apartment until it passed, the air sweeping into me like some kind of cleansing light, pushing out thoughts about voices and solitude and the possibility of living a different kind of life.

"How long have you been here?" I asked.

"Hours," he said. "They gave me a Coke a little while ago."

I sat across from him. "Is what they're telling me true?"

"What are they telling you?"

"That you hit two city workers in the legs with a flashlight."

"I pushed one of them into the wet concrete they were using to seal the tunnel. I wonder if he got stuck there." He sighed and I smelled the sweetness of soda on his breath. "Then the police brought me here and said they had to call my parents or guardian and I told them I only had you."

"What did I say about using that flashlight, Denver?"

"It was an emergency," he protested. "They were filling up my tunnel. I spent all morning drawing a map of the other side of the world. I was going to find important things there." He rubbed his elbow and sniffed. "I heard this grinding noise and I went outside and these guys were making my tunnel disappear."

"Fuck, Denver." I cradled my forehead in my palm. At the funeral, the family members had taken turns sprinkling dirt onto the coffins. When it was my brother's turn, he whipped a rubber dagger out of his suit jacket. He raised the slate-colored blade toward the clouds, then dropped it into my father's grave. They'll need it, he said before skulking over to an oak tree on the edge of the cemetery, where he remained for the rest of the service.

"Am I going to jail?"

"No." From the shrillness of his voice, I could tell he was about to cry. "Or at least I don't think so. We'll probably be fined or something. We can ask Aunt Lucille for extra money."

He nodded. We were quiet for a while. He kept wiping his nose on the underside of his wrist. I was waiting for someone to walk into the room and tell us what we needed to do in order to leave, but no one came. I wanted to see the sky again, the tree branches and the leaves that were beginning to curl from the heat. I wanted to lead us away from here.

"Question." I pressed my hands against the table. "Do you know anyone named Calvin?"

"A kid in my second grade class went by Calvin." His face tensed with concentration. "Is that who you mean?"

"It would be someone older, someone Mom and Dad knew." His posture stiffened when I mentioned our parents, but I kept going. "Do you know who I'm talking about?"

"No," he said. "I don't."

I stood and paced in slow circles. "I might have to find a new job."

"Why?"

"It's too hard to explain."

"You always say that." The high pitch returned to his voice. "You never want to explain anything to me."

"I know," I told him. "I'm sorry."

He covered his face with his forearm. I continued walking in circles. The floor was sticky and gray. When the door opened, I stopped and looked at Denver. He was still shielding his eyes, oblivious to our new company, the social worker I had spoken with earlier and a police officer. The social worker glanced at my brother and told me to sit down. I stayed on my feet. She started talking about paperwork and evaluations and probation and I struggled to grab her words. They bounced around the room like echoes in a canyon. Or the lightning bugs Denver and I used to chase in the backyard, our parents' silhouettes filling the tall windows of the house, our fingers reaching for the glow that came and went.

we are calling to offer you
a fabulous life

L ast night, Joyce was mugged. She was locking up Darnel's shop in the East Village when a man drifted out of an alley and ripped her purse from her shoulder. She never got a clear view of his face, just a glimpse of his profile and then a long look at his squat figure charging down the sidewalk, her little black purse dangling from his wrist. She had felt the impulse to scream, but only a low hiccup passed through her lips. Her apartment keys were tucked inside her coat pocket and she'd slapped her hip just to make sure, feeling the metal shapes through the fabric. It wasn't an expensive purse, but she'd carried it every day for the last two years and couldn't help but feel that she'd suffered a loss.

She told all of this to Darnel at The Mask Market the next afternoon, sitting on a stool behind the cash register. He stood across from her, the glass display case between them. His hair was slicked back; he had a few days of stubble on his cheeks and chin. The store carried tribal art and textiles, specializing in Indonesian masks. Joyce had been working there for five months. She was only two weeks into the job when Darnel started taking her to lunch and grazing her back or waist when he slipped by to reach the register or lift a mask off the wall. At first, they just locked the shop door and went into the back and lay down amongst the wood figures and uneven towers of cardboard boxes. Then they began sneaking off to her apartment, which Joyce liked best—the feeling of having someone in her bed, walking naked through her kitchen and pouring a glass of water, as though he might have lived there. He would tell her about Bali, where he went twice a year for merchandise. He had even talked about bringing her along on his next buying trip, about watching late night topeng dances and snorkeling and swimming naked in the sea.

"That doesn't really qualify as a mugging," Darnel said after Joyce finished her story.

"All right." She shifted on the stool, crossing and uncrossing her skinny legs. "What would you call it?"

"A purse snatching." He looked at her and shrugged. "A mugging involves a weapon of some sort. A knife or a gun."

"I had to cancel my credit card and order a replacement," she said. "And he gave me a hard push before he started running." That wasn't true, but sometimes she couldn't resist a chance to make Darnel feel guilty.

"You're lucky." He walked around the display case and put his arm over her shoulder. "Lucky you weren't shot or beaten or worse."

"I guess," she said, even though she didn't feel lucky at all. She had wanted to call Darnel the moment she got home and ask him to come over, but knew it was far too late to phone without arousing his wife's suspicion. Instead she turned her noise machine to Evening Monsoon and slept with the lights on and got up in the middle of the night to make sure the door was locked.

"I wish I'd been there, Joyce." He gave her a squeeze. "I really do."

"Will you come by before closing?"

"How about later tonight? I'll call your apartment." He tapped the large face of his wristwatch. "Andrea has a Lamaze class at three."

Darnel's wife was six months pregnant. She had come by the shop last month, saying she'd been in the neighborhood and wanted to check on the merchandise. It was the first time Joyce had seen her. She had a round face and squinty eyes, her stomach protruding underneath a pink cotton blouse. After she walked through the store and spent a minute rustling around in the back, Joyce noticed how unbalanced she looked, on the brink of toppling over, and offered her the stool to sit on, but she only shook her head, said the masks were dirty, and then left. That same afternoon, Joyce sat on a box of ceramic bowls in the back and wrote Darnel a letter, telling him they couldn't possibly continue under these circumstances. *What am I doing here?* she wrote. *I can't understand what I'm doing with my life.* She even sealed and stamped the letter, but was never able to drop it into the mailbox. It was still in her apartment, in the top drawer of her dresser, underneath a pile of winter socks.

"I won't be too late," he said, releasing her shoulders. "Maybe we could even get dinner."

Joyce slumped on the stool. The shop smelled of incense and mothballs. Last night, after the culprit was out of sight, she'd leaned against the store window, the glass cool against her face, and felt the glare of the masks. When Joyce began working at the shop, the masks had terrified her, all those bulging wooden eyes and flung open mouths, the painted faces that, during the evening shifts, radiated an eerie light. Most were shaded red, green, blue, and gold, the eyes silver or black, some decorated with feathers or tufts of human hair, the most expensive ones studded with semiprecious stones: lapis, charoite, gaspeite, jasper. The death masks resembled human faces, the eyes and lips exaggerated into menacing caricatures, while the others were designed to look like animals, painted whiskers and long white tusks. After the mugging, Joyce focused on one mask in particular: the death mask that hung right above the register. It was the largest piece in the shop, painted acid greens and blues, with huge red eyes and white teeth. She'd stared at the mask through the window for a long time, as though it could offer her some kind of rescue.

"Can we go to the café down the street?" Joyce asked.

Darnel kissed the top of her head. "Whatever you like."

She walked him outside and watched him move down the sidewalk, his lumbering steps. It was spring. The trees were tipped with green and white. The brick façade of the building across the street was covered in blue and gray graffiti and the colors looked almost cheerful in the sunlight. Every so often, someone would get stuck behind Darnel's broad frame and lurch left and right, looking for a way to pass. It had always seemed strange to her, the way people hurried even when they had no particular destination in mind.

Joyce went back inside and dusted the masks, standing on the stool to reach the ones that hung closer to the ceiling, as she did every afternoon, despite what Darnel's wife had said. During the rest of her shift, she only had three customers. First, an older woman wearing a caftan and white braces on her wrists. She didn't say anything to Joyce when she came into the store, just stood in the center of the room for a little while and gazed at the walls of masks, her mouth tight with confusion, as though this wasn't where she had meant to end up. An hour later, a couple lingered in front of a death mask that cost several hundred dollars. They both wore shorts and sandals and carried mesh tote bags. The spoke in a foreign language; the man kept touching the space between the woman's shoulders. Joyce watched them from behind the register. They were young, early twenties, and looked happy. She both envied and pitied them.

The woman pointed at the display case, which held a selection of semiprecious stones. Garnet, red jasper, moonstone, tourmaline. She asked Joyce which types were supposed to bring luck in love. Joyce opened the case and took out an opal. The stone was shaped like a small egg. In the woman's slender hands, it gleamed blue.

"This one is good for love," Joyce said. "But I have something even better." She handed the woman a piece of unakite. It was a rough stone, speckled with green and pink. Unakite, she told the woman, was supposed to help with finding direction. If you ground the stone and then looked into the powder, you would know what you needed to do. Joyce had considered grinding the stone for herself; once, after finding a mortar and pestle in the back, she placed some unakite in the bowl, but she couldn't bring herself to crush it, afraid it would reveal she'd taken too many wrong turns to get back on track, or, worse, that it wouldn't tell her anything at all. She hoped this woman would be braver.

"Here," she said, returning the opal to the case and closing the woman's hand around the other stone. "This is the one you really want."

After Joyce's shift, she took the subway to The Fish Emporium on 8ᵗʰ Street. Earlier in the day, she had used the store computer to look up photos of fish found in Bali—angelfishes and clownfishes and blacktip groupers—and decided it was time she got herself a pet. Bali. Whenever she walked down the street or hung onto the handles that dangled from the tops of subway cars, she repeated the word to herself like a song. Bali, Bali, Bali. The first time Darnel mentioned going to Bali, the idea hooked itself into her immediately. She bought a map, which she sometimes unrolled on her bed, so she could study the shape of the island; if work was slow, she used the computer to find pictures of Bali, mist-covered mountain ranges and azure waters and temples with roofs shaped like giant jenga puzzles. When she saw something about Bali, an ad for a resort or a travel article, she tore out the pages. She had never traveled outside the United States, not even on her honeymoon with her ex-husband (they had gone to a bed-and-breakfast in Maine). She thought this was symptomatic of something, though she wasn't sure what.

Joyce had moved to Manhattan from upstate New York after her marriage broke up six months ago. She was married for five years. When she first met her husband, he was living with another woman. She was almost a decade older than Joyce, a retired ballerina who taught dance at a private girls' school. Her husband had lived with the ballerina for eight years, longer than Joyce and he ended up being married, and after they had divorced, Joyce realized she'd never gotten over the feeling that their marriage had been poisoned by the betrayal on which their life together was founded.

She had been surprised by how easy it was to leave. She told him the morning after they got into an argument over a movie they'd seen. At the end of the movie, the heroine walked into the sea and drowned herself in order to escape her monotonous life in a Norwegian fishing village. Joyce found her choice noble, while her husband thought it absurd, and, over dinner at the same Italian restaurant they always frequented, they argued their cases bitterly, skimming the edges of bigger, knottier issues that they could not articulate or even really understand. They went to bed angry and, in the middle of the night, Joyce woke with an ache in her chest and wandered into the guest room to sleep. When she went downstairs the next morning, her husband was sitting at the kitchen table with his bran flakes and newspaper, slurping the milk like he always did. She sat down and told him that she no longer wanted to fall asleep and wake with his body next to hers. He looked at her, his face expressionless except for his eyes—his pupils, she could have sworn, widened like spilled ink. Then he flipped to the sports section and went back to eating his bran flakes. And that was that.

During the divorce, when her friends and family asked what had happened, Joyce said the marriage had simply run its course, as if losing a husband were no less complicated than quitting a tedious job. But in truth, the separation, the sudden rush of solitude, had left her feeling like she'd misplaced some part of herself in a foreign land. It wasn't that she missed her husband, but that the divorce hadn't brought the relief, the clarity, she desired. The one thing she did know is that she was glad to get out of upstate New York. She'd always disliked her job in real estate—she never got the hang of sales pitches and was usually only allowed to show rentals—and the stillness of the suburbs, the quiet routines of her neighbors, people waiting for their lives to get better or worse or end. She signed a lease for the first apartment she saw, a one bedroom in Alphabet City, and found her job in the classified section of the *New York Sun*. Her friends were horrified to discover that Joyce, a licensed real estate agent, was working in a tribal art store for an hourly wage, but Joyce felt she no longer belonged in the world of 401Ks and home ownership. She just needed to duck underneath the surface long enough to figure a few things out.

The inside of The Fish Emporium was cool and dark. The walls were lined with tanks that glowed a phosphorescent blue. At first, Joyce thought the store was empty. The doors chimed when she entered, but it took several minutes for a young woman, with cropped blonde hair and stacks of silver rings on her fingers, to appear.

"Sorry," the woman said. "Business has been slow ever since *New York Times Magazine* ran an article that called fish passé pets for city kids."

"I don't think fish are passé," Joyce said.

"Me either," the woman said. "In fact, I love them."

She took Joyce by the elbow and showed her the selections of butterflyfish and algae eaters and Japanese fighting fish, beautiful, velvety-scaled creatures that had to be kept in individual tanks.

"If you get two of these and put their fishbowls side by side, they'll spend all day staring at each other," the woman said. When they passed a tank of goldfish, Joyce was reminded of the orange anthias that swam in Bali's reefs. She peered into the tank and watched the fat orange fish dart through the water.

"I'll take one of those," she said.

When the woman plunged the little green net into the water, all the fish darted away. After a few swings, she scooped up a fish with a white spot on its side and dumped into a plastic bag filled with water. Before Joyce left, she picked out a top-of-the-line brand of pellets, a glass fishbowl, and a little plastic castle to go inside.

In her apartment, Joyce placed the glass bowl in the bedroom windowsill and emptied the plastic bag into it. She watched the fish bob around in the water and circle the pink castle. She set the noise machine on her bedside table to Midnight Mist, then kneeled on the floor and stared at the fish's black eyes and orange scales, its tail in the shape of wings. For a moment, she wished she could call her husband into the room to watch the tiny air bubbles rise from the fish's mouth to the top of the bowl like miniature balloons. But she knew, if he were here, that he wouldn't sit on the floor and watch the fish with her. He would think it was a silly and pointless way to pass time, and that was why she had left.

Later that evening, it started to rain. Joyce showered and changed into a sleeveless silk dress with yellow flowers printed on the front. She cleaned her apartment and set the noise machine to Rainforest Chatter. By eight o'clock, the goldfish had figured out how to swim through the circular hole in the center of the castle and Joyce had given up on Darnel coming in time for dinner. She ate leftover takeout, sitting on the bed and looking into the fishbowl. She was looking forward to showing him the goldfish and telling him she'd picked this one because it reminded her of the anthias that lived in the waters of Bali, which, if they ever went snorkeling like he said they would, they'd see huge schools of near the reefs.

At ten, Joyce was about to exchange her dress for running shorts and a T-shirt when Darnel called and said he would be there soon.

"It's late," Joyce said when he finally arrived, his hair damp from the rain. "What did you tell your wife?"

"That there was a problem at the shop." Darnel smiled and pinched her wrist. "Which isn't a total lie."

"Ha," Joyce said. "Ha, ha, ha."

He wasted no time unzipping her dress. He stroked her back, pressing her body into his. His hands were wide and hot and she felt consumed by them. She kissed him, leaning against a wall. He unzipped his pants and lifted the hem of her dress.

When it was over, they lay on her bed for a while. The sound of dripping water came from the noise machine. She turned away from Darnel, but could still feel the warm, damp line of his body against her. Would she want to fall asleep and wake with him every day and night? She was considering this question when Darnel noticed the goldfish.

"What's its name?" he asked.

"Bali." She hoped he'd say something about an upcoming trip, but he only sighed and told her that he wouldn't be able to stay much longer.

Joyce watched the goldfish lap the castle, running her fingers over the spines of the books sitting on her bedside table, underneath the nose machine. They were on the history of Indonesian tribal art. Darnel had lent them to her, so she could learn about the merchandise and answer questions for customers. One book described how the masks were carved: flat chisels and gouges created the first ridges and curves, then double-edged knives refined the features and hollowed out the inside of the mask. The death masks protected the deceased during their passage into the underworld. Many death mask eyes were reinforced with a layer of human bone on the inside; the blocked eyes were supposed to prevent harmful spirits from entering the body. And much of the power lay in the stones: jasper could end droughts; lapis kept away troubling dreams; opal attracted love. The mask makers had to follow the strict conventions issued by the tribes, precise patterns of coloring and carving, or else risk being cast out of the tribe and, some believed, angering the spirit power of the mask. Joyce's reading made her feel uneasy about people buying the masks and hanging them in their homes without knowing the capabilities of their new acquisitions.

"Do you ever worry about the people you sell masks to?" Joyce asked.

"What do you mean?"

"What if a mask brought them bad luck?"

"Then they'd have to buy another one that brought them better luck."

She could tell he was getting restless from the way he was shifting around on the bed.

"I should leave," Darnel said, sitting up. "Andrea has a morning appointment."

"Tell me one thing about Bali before you go," she said. He leaned over her and brushed hair from the side of her face. She felt his breath against her ear. He told her about Mount Agung, Bali's highest summit. The Balinese believed gods lived on the mountaintop. If you climbed to the peak of the mountain, you were supposed to be able to see into your own soul, and because of this most people who reached the top never returned.

In the middle of the night, Joyce was woken by a ringing phone. It took her some time to realize the sound was coming from her own apartment. She kicked away the covers and lurched into the kitchen, her mind sticky with sleep, and answered.

"Am I speaking to the primary resident?" It was a woman, the voice high-pitched and strange.

"Yes."

"Are there any other residents?"

"No."

"Not even a cat or a dog?"

"No."

"A goldfish?"

"Actually, yes." Joyce rested a hand on the counter. The rain was still falling outside. It pained her to think of how long it had been since she'd had a phone conversation with someone besides Darnel. "As of today, there is a goldfish."

"Still," the caller said. "You must be lonely."

She looked around the kitchen, which was barely large enough to hold a mini-refrigerator and a microwave. The sink had been clogged for a week, but she hadn't taken any steps to repair it, ordering most of her meals from the Chinese restaurant below her apartment and eating out of the cardboard containers.

"Hello, sole resident," the woman said. "Are you still with me?"

"If you'll tell me what you want." As a teenager, she had played phone games with neighborhood girls on Saturday nights. They would open the phone book, close their eyes, and point to a name. Joyce knew this call was probably just a prank, just kids looking to make fun of a woman alone in the city, but maybe, she allowed herself to believe for a moment, it was something else entirely.

"The rain is melting the city," the woman said. "Are you melted yet?"

"Not yet," Joyce replied. "Maybe I'm a penguin."

"You're no penguin. Not a polar bear either."

"How do you know?" She walked to the window and pulled back the curtains. The street was quiet. It was dawning on her that a strange call in the middle of the night should be making her nervous. "You're just a stranger on the phone."

"I'm a specialist."

"In what?"

"All things."

"So why are you calling me?"

"To offer you something."

"And what's that?" Her voice sharpened. "What could you offer me?" There was a burst of laughter in the background, followed by a low thump. Perhaps, she thought, it was one of the teenagers who waited tables downstairs, playing some kind of joke.

"We are calling," the woman said, "to offer you a fabulous life."

Joyce heard a click, the buzz of the dial tone. She looked out the window again before unplugging the phone. She put the noise machine on Roaring River, then turned on all the lights in her apartment and sat on the floor. She didn't understand what had just happened, why she had kept talking, what the woman had meant by all the things she said. She felt dazed. She watched the goldfish swim from one side of the bowl to the other.

"I don't understand this world," Joyce said to her fish.

The next afternoon, Darnel came to the shop and told Joyce they needed to talk. She was on a stepladder, straightening one of the masks. She had never gone back to sleep after the phone call and felt exhausted.

"About what?" she asked, not looking at him.

"Let's get some lunch," Darnel said.

Joyce got off the ladder and turned to Darnel. He held a large white envelope in his arms. The top three buttons of his dark blue silk shirt were undone, which Joyce thought looked a little ridiculous. She could hardly believe this was the same man who'd whispered in her ear the night before.

"What's in the envelope?" she asked.

"I'll show you when we're sitting down," he said.

He did not kiss her on the lips, did not hug her and dig his fingers into the muscle of her back or suggest they swing by her apartment after lunch. She locked up the store and then they walked to a café down the street. It was humid outside, the clouds rimmed with black.

At the café, they sat outside. She stared at the envelope, the unlikeliest of possibilities flooding her mind: it contained travel brochures, two tickets to Bali, he was about to propose their escape.

After the waitress took their order, Darnel placed the envelope on the table. Joyce tugged one of her pearl earrings and watched the sidewalk. The pearls were tiny and fake and pinched her skin if she wore them for too long. A man passed the café, shouting into his cell phone. A woman walked by seconds later, a hardcover book pressed against her chest, as though she was holding a child.

"Are you ready to show me what's in the envelope?" she asked.

"Are you ready to see it?"

She shrugged. The waitress reappeared with their order. Joyce added cream to her coffee and took a sip. One of her favorite moments of the day was watching the splash of cream dissolve into her coffee, the little white swirl, a small luxury.

He pulled out a large photograph and handed it to Joyce. The background was dark, with a fan of paleness in the center and a figure trapped inside the light.

"The first picture," he said. "A boy."

"Great," she said. "That's all the world needs."

The shape of the baby resembled a giant olive, the features and limbs fuzzy. Thoughts of Bali evaporated like mist being burned away by a rising sun. She wanted to tear the picture in half, to dump her coffee over that tunnel of light. But she could not stop staring into the waves of black and gray and the lump in the center. Finally, Darnel took the sonogram from her and returned it to the envelope. They were both quiet for a while. She finished her coffee. He drank his beer and ate his cheeseburger.

"I'll give you as long as you need to find another job," he said.

"I'll only need a few days," she said. "To find something else." She was already dreading facing the Bali pages she'd pinned to her refrigerator, evidence of her stupidity, of her inevitable humiliation. She asked Darnel if he wanted his books back. He did not.

"I'd appreciate a quick exit," he said. "But I understand your position."

"You couldn't possibly."

"I'll get lunch."

"How noble of you." Joyce tried to think of the Evening Surf setting on her noise machine, the lulling sound of water hitting sand. Then she told Darnel something she'd never said to anyone before, that the thing she missed most about being married was the actual word "marriage," being able to say she was "in a marriage" or "working on her marriage." It gave her the feeling of being a part of something that mattered, something vital and alive.

"But I wasn't a part of something that mattered," she said. "And neither are you."

"I was worried you might cry," he said. "But I think the way you're acting now is even worse."

"And how is that? How am I acting?"

"Like you're going to stab me with your fork the moment I turn around."

"I wish I had it in me." She stood and dropped her napkin onto the table.

"Are you going back to the shop?"

"Yes."

"I'll come by later to see how you're doing," he said.

She began to walk away, then stopped and looked back. Darnel was hunched in his chair, staring down at his empty plate. What I really want, she thought, is to not want to want him to chase after me. She left the café and started down the sidewalk. The sky was the same dull gray. She passed the red and yellow awning of a meat market, a restaurant with paper pineapples and bananas hanging from the ceiling, walls of graffiti.

When Joyce entered the shop, she immediately felt the glare of the masks, weighty and sharp, as though they knew what had happened, or had seen it all happen before. She stood in the center of the store, surrounded by swirls of color, the glint of stones, hollow eyes and wild grins. She found the mask that hung behind the display case, the one that had leapt into her mind after her purse was taken and the man disappeared into the shadowed street; the stark white teeth and red eyes, the forehead studded with onyx and amazonite.

She went behind the case and stood on a stool. She was surprised by the weight of the mask when she lifted it from the wall; it stretched from her neck to her hips. She placed it on the glass surface of the case and studied the expression, the subtle blending of colors, the points where the paint thickened slightly. She raised the mask to her face and felt the smoothness of the wood.

Darnel hadn't come by the shop and she didn't expect he would. He was probably back with his wife, a hand resting on her puffy stomach. She took twenty dollars from the register, for the cab she would call to carry her and the mask away from the shop. The theft made her giddy. She went into the front and stretched out on the carpet. She felt consoled by all the faces, an audience for her life. She lay straight as a corpse and watched the ceiling fan spin in lazy circles, the low hum muffled by the noise on the street.

In the taxi, Joyce asked the driver to drop her at Tompkins Square Park. She wasn't quite ready to return home. The mask was balanced across her lap, the red eyes staring up at her, perfectly circular and the size of plums. The cab docked on the curb and Joyce handed the driver the twenty and told him to keep the change. The humidity made the loose strands of hair around her face curl; the air was sticky and thick against her skin.

She followed the wide concrete path, passing stands of elms, the branches curved and heavy with foliage, and oriental planes, the pointed leaves brushing the ground. The mask was difficult to carry and she kept having to reposition her hands to keep a good grip, but she didn't mind. She liked having it close to her. The park was nearly empty: a young woman sitting on a bench and reading a paperback, a man sleeping on the ground, a sheet of cardboard covering his arms and torso.

Joyce stopped walking when she reached a fountain carved from pale stone, a memorial for the Slocum disaster, a boating accident in the East River that killed nearly a thousand people in the early nineteen hundreds. The fountain smelled of sulfur. She watched water pour from the parted mouth of a lion, the stone eyes and mane shaped in a way that reminded her of the wood figures in the shop. She held the mask in front of her stomach and wrapped her arms around it.

She was standing by the fountain when she heard the boy's voice behind her. He said to turn around and she did.

The hood of his sweatshirt was pulled over his head and his face was angled towards the ground, but she was able to see a clump of stringy blonde hair and a pimple on his cheek. He flinched a little when he saw the mask. It took her a minute to comprehend what was happening, to notice his hand underneath the front of his sweatshirt, the nose of the gun pressing against the fabric. He told her to give him everything and she simply shook her head.

"I don't have anything," she said, looking over his shoulder. "No money." The open circle in the park was empty, the space surrounded by trees and bushes, the branches thick and green. She listened carefully for voices or footsteps, but heard nothing. She looked at the boy. Twice in the same week. She could not believe it.

"What about that?" He gestured towards the mask with his gun. "That's got to be worth something."

"Yes," she said. "It's worth quite a lot."

He moved closer, head still lowered. She smelled cigarettes on his breath, saw sweat on the bridge of his nose. She gripped the edges of the mask, her fingers throbbing. He pushed his hand forward, so she could see the outline of the gun even more clearly. "Last chance," he said.

It was then Joyce started to laugh. She had meant to scream, but the noise that spilled from her mouth was piercing laughter. Her face was hot, her sides knotted and aching. She tried to think of things that were not, in any way, funny: the boy pulling the gun out from underneath his sweatshirt and pressing it against her forehead, the mask shattering on the ground, Darnel's bloated, listless wife. But Bali kept coming into her mind. Bali! How could she have possibly believed Darnel would take her to someplace like Bali? It was all so ridiculous, and she kept going.

The boy jerked his head. His hood slipped back. For a moment, she saw his eyes: a cloudy gray-blue, confused and frightened as the possums that sometimes wandered into the roads of upstate New York. She laughed harder. Something in her chest was tightening, closing, and she began to get dizzy. When the boy raised his chin and looked into her eyes, she thought she was dead. All she could see in her mind was the mask; she imagined it settling on her face, the weight and scent of the wood. But the boy relaxed his arm, turned, and ran down the path, one hand still fixed in front of his stomach, the back of his sweatshirt flapping like a cape.

After the boy disappeared, Joyce set the mask down and waited by the fountain until she was sure he was really gone. Given all that had happened, she felt strangely unshaken. She picked up the mask and began walking. She passed a corner grocery store, boxes of tomatoes and bundles of yellow tulips on display outside, and a sex shop, the mannequins dressed in pink wigs and lingerie staring dumbly through the glass.

She went to her street and entered the Chinese restaurant on the ground floor of her building, where she requested pork dumplings and moo shu chicken. The waiters paused to stare at the mask; the customers looked up from their plates, mouths bulging with food. She felt powerful and exotic. Her order came quickly, dots of grease already expanding across the brown paper bag when they handed it to her.

One of the busboys stopped, a lanky kid with a scar on his cheek, a white tub of dishes pressed against his hip. He nodded at the mask. "Who's your friend?"

"Isn't he lovely," Joyce said. She wondered if the boy had been involved with the call to her apartment. "He puts hexes on people at random."

"That should come in handy," he replied before slipping into the kitchen.

In her apartment, Joyce placed the mask on her bed and put the noise machine on Summer Monsoon, then sat on the floor, near the fishbowl. She opened the container of dumplings and ate them with her fingers, flipping through the classifieds in the *New York Sun*. She read the job listings aloud to her fish: data entry in Brooklyn, a call for a translator of Turkish in Queens, a receptionist at a nail salon in the West Village. She couldn't go back to where she had come from, but she didn't think she could stay where she was either. She would have to find a way forward, towards that gray line on the horizon.

She set aside the newspaper and the dumplings and looked at the mask. While waiting for the cab, she'd considered leaving the shop door unlocked or maybe even propped open, but it saddened her to think of the masks being stolen or vandalized. Darnel had been counting on her to close tonight and probably wouldn't return to the store until morning. She wondered what he would do when he found the mask missing. Come to her apartment, call the police. Or just let it go. It had cost him some money in Bali; the price tag said eight hundred dollars, although that was probably twice what he paid. Maybe he'd be so glad she went quietly, he would be willing to accept the loss.

It was dusk. The city lights beamed; the sallow moon hung needlessly in the sky. Joyce thought she heard the faint ring of a phone and imagined her anonymous caller dialing the number of another apartment, grabbing someone else's life by the throat and shaking it. She pressed her hands over the mask's white teeth, as though she was keeping something from leaking out. The onyx and amazonite glistened like drops of black and turquoise paint. She considered taking it to the library tomorrow and checking out more books about death masks and their powers. She only knew they were supposed to transform the wearer in the afterlife, to make them braver and luckier and happier, to help them find their way through a new kind of world.

inverness

All evening, the men spoke only of the monster. Although I sat at their table in the quaint hotel bar—known as the malt shop, due to the hundreds of malt whiskey selections—and was a scientist myself, I wasn't a part of the conversation. In truth, I thought their pursuit unworthy. The four scientists had been commissioned by the BBC to debunk the legend of the Loch Ness Monster, while I, a botanist who specialized in the preservation of endangered plant life, was working with the Botany Institute of Britain to perform field research on rare plants.

I had been in Inverness for a week and had experienced little contact with anyone at the Craigdarroch except Sarah, the proprietor, and the monster hunters, as they were called. Three of the men were from London. The fourth man, McKay, operated the mini-submarine, a steel contraption that resembled a large gray egg. He was a native of Inverness, a local expert on the Loch Ness Monster, and had learned about submarine technology as a young man, during his army days. He dressed shabbily, his pants often torn at the knees, and whenever he checked the time, it was his practice to take out his pocket watch and swing it in front of his face, as though he was trying to hypnotize himself. He was also Sarah's husband. They'd been married for fifteen years. This afternoon, when I returned to the Craigdarroch after a day of field work, I'd come upon them arguing in the lobby. Their voices were low, but there was tension in their expressions, in the sweeping gestures of their arms. They fell silent after seeing me in the lobby, and I'd hurried past them and up the stairs.

That night, as I drank my second glass of merlot, I listed to the men, who were outfitted with sonar sensors and giant nets and aquatic cameras, discuss their findings. Or, as it were, the lack thereof.

"The sonars have picked up nothing," Ian said, adjusting his round eyeglasses. "Not even the slightest disturbance in the water."

"Did you actually think you were going to find a plesiosaur?" Theodore emptied his glass before turning to me. He was the tallest of the men, with a long nose and high cheekbones. "The most common Loch Ness theory proposes the monster is a plesiosaur, a species that was extinct sixty million years ago."

"An elasmosaur," Dale said. "A member of the plesiosaur family." He was the shortest of the scientists and wore flannel shirts with the sleeves cuffed to his elbows. "And they became extinct seventy million years ago. Not sixty."

The Loch Ness Monster—although I'd given it little thought before coming to Inverness—now seemed much like the fog that hung over the lake and hills: suggestive and hazy and constantly present. The locals lived peacefully with the legend, profited from it even, with gift shops that carried Loch Ness Monster tee-shirts and coffee mugs.

Theodore stood, knocking back his chair, and skulked over to the bar for a refill. Sarah was working in the malt shop that evening, occasionally refilling our glasses and polishing the mahogany bar. After tending to Theodore, she pulled a chair up to our table; when our eyes met, she smiled. We were, for the time being, the only women residing in the Craigdarroch.

It was then McKay looked across the table at me and said, "They aren't underwater like I am. Nothing shows up on the sonar, that's true, but near the bottom of the lake, I'm telling you, there's something strange."

"He's never been able to stay away from the Loch," Sarah said. She was petite and fair, her cheeks ruddy from the weather. Her wedding ring was a plain gold band which, I'd noticed, she had a habit of pushing around her finger. "I joke that it's his first love."

"Why don't you tell Emily about the underwater caves," Theodore said, raising his glass. "Maybe that's where Nessie is waiting."

"You should go down with me sometime."

Theodore shook his head. "I prefer dry land."

"Have you ever been down with him, Sarah?" I asked.

"No." She reached across the table and picked up McKay's beer. She held it in her hands for a moment before taking a sip. "I suppose I prefer dry land too."

"Are there really underwater caves?" I imagined dark holes where aquatic weeds and ferns flourished, hornwort and eelgrass clinging to slippery gray rocks.

"Yes," Ian said. "There are."

"But our sonars are so sensitive, if there were anything in the caves, we'd know," Dale said.

"Absolutely," Theodore said.

Ian nodded. "Without a doubt."

"You think you know so much," McKay said. "You think everything can be measured."

Sarah began to say something, but he shook his head and she stopped. He said that he didn't want to start an argument, that he'd said all he had to say for tonight. True to his word, he did not speak for the rest of the evening.

After we decided to retire, he helped Sarah clear away the glasses. When they were both behind the bar, I noticed her pausing to touch the space between his shoulder blades, or to run a hand down the side of his body. He had a strange way of polishing glasses. He jammed the little towel inside and twisted it around, then held the glass to the light and repeated his method three or four times before adding the glass to the shelf, as though he was able to see imperfections that weren't visible to the rest of us.

Later that night, back in my room, I listened for the bagpipes. The music usually began around midnight and ceased at two in the morning. When the weather is good, Sarah had said while checking me into the Craigdarroch last week, a trio of bagpipers stand on the edge of the Loch and play in hopes of rousing the monster. On some nights, I'd closed my eyes and listened so intently that, for a moment, I mistook the music for a prolonged and ragged wail.

The Inverness weather was the perfect habitat for what I was seeking: the *Linnaea borealis*, or twinflower. I should have felt exhilarated by the variety of plant species that thrived in the lush forests and by the esteemed botanists on the research team (all of whom were from Scotland or elsewhere in the UK and, if not ensconced in their own homes, staying with friends or relatives; I was the only one in need of a hotel). The population of twinflowers had declined in recent years, due to an increase in the mechanical harvesting of timber, but even in the protected areas, they still weren't flourishing, and I had been given the opportunity to help understand why life had become such a struggle for them. Yet I could not shake the loneliness that had settled in months earlier and clung as stubbornly as the fog to the hilltops.

I had called Peter once since coming to Inverness, sitting at a desk in the corner of my room and staring out the window, bending my calling card in my hand. He had left me three months ago, though I was often surprised by how much time had passed, the pain still so immediate. When the phone rang and Peter's answering machine came on, I breathed into the receiver and struggled to think of something casual yet significant to say, all the while watching McKay's mini-submarine gradually emerge in the center of the lake. Water slid off the dark metal and, in the later afternoon sunlight, the machine gleamed. I hung up the phone without leaving anything on the machine except the sound of my breath, too transfixed by the movements of the submarine to feel the sense of defeat and embarrassment that would descend upon me later in the day.

Lying on my back in bed, the covers bunched around my waist, I thought of the underwater caves hidden in the Loch, of McKay piloting the submarine into one of the caverns, his face tightening as the water darkened and shadows passed over the submarine. He was odd-looking, slight and a little dead-eyed, a contrast to Sarah's airy beauty. But there was something electric about him too, something inviting. I wondered if he was frightened when the submarine disappeared beneath the surface, or if a part of him wanted to remain there always.

In the morning, before Sarah delivered me to Reelig Glen, where I would continue my search for the twinflower, I took a walk along the bank of the Loch. The fog was thickest in the morning and after drifting farther from the hotel, I realized the white haze had surrounded me. I knew I was late for work; in the distance, I thought I heard Sarah calling my name. I kept walking.

D.C. always looked hazy at the start of the day, although it was not white like the fog of Scotland, but gray, a mixture of early morning mist and smog. After leaving our DuPont Circle apartment in the mornings, Peter and I would go to a coffee shop for tea and pastries, then ride the metro to Georgetown University, where we taught in the graduate programs. We had lived together for four years. For a long time, I had believed we would one day marry.

I stopped to pick up an object lying in the dirt: a portion of a cigar, damp and leafy, the tip bitten down to a dull point. Left by one of the bagpipers, I assumed, inhaling the scent before flicking it back onto the ground. When I rose and stepped forward, the shock of the wetness, which traveled halfway up my calf, sent me reeling backwards, landing on the bank of the lake. Through the fog, I could not see where water met shore, but I surely had gone farther than intended. I jumped up and walked briskly toward the Craigdarroch. My breathing slowed as the landscape became more visible, the hills and mountain peaks. Once I was free of the densest fog, I spotted a figure approaching the lake. I raised a hand. The person stopped, but didn't gesture toward me. When I was close enough to recognize McKay's face, I called out his name.

His hair was more disheveled than usual, his hooded eyes rimmed with pink. He didn't speak until we were face to face, until he looked down at the dark leg of my jeans.

"What were you doing out there?"

"Went for a walk," I said. "I couldn't see properly."

"Looks like you got too close to the edge. Not sure I'd do that again."

"I've heard the Loch Ness Monster lives deep in the lake, that it never attacks people on the shore."

"Then you haven't heard all the stories."

"What have you planned for this week?" I asked.

"We'll be reviewing new data and doing repairs for the next two days," he said. "And then I'm taking the submarine to the bottom of Urquhart Bay."

I was familiar with that section of the Loch. I often passed the ruins of Urquhart Castle, which overlooked the lake, while leaving and returning to the Craigdarroch.

"It's the last step," he continued. "Going to the bottom."

"Then it's all over?"

"If we find nothing, the others pack up and go home."

"How long have they been in Inverness?"

"Eight weeks." He paused, pushed a hand into the back pocket of his jeans. "The lake is twenty-one miles long and a mile wide. Two months was barely enough."

I looked toward the Craigdarroch and saw Sarah standing by her van, waving. After I waved back, she pointed at her wristwatch and then raised her arms.

"Late for the laboratory?" McKay asked.

I nodded. "The other members of my research team work in the mornings. Your wife has been kind enough to drive me."

"What are you looking for?"

"The twinflower." I described the appearance of the flower, two bell-shaped blossoms that hang from a slender stem. "They're very rare now, so I suppose I'm looking for the extraordinary."

McKay smiled a little before turning away. "Aren't we all."

I watched until he disappeared into the fog like an apparition, never once looking back at me or his wife. I walked over to Sarah's maroon van and climbed into the passenger seat. My wet pant leg stuck to my skin, the denim cold and rough.

"Sorry to be so slow." I pointed at my jeans. "I had a mishap at the lake."

She started the car. "Hopefully it didn't involve anything that would require the attention of the monster hunters."

"No," I said. "Just my own clumsiness."

"I don't go down to the water very often," she said. "That's my husband's territory."

I mentioned McKay had just been telling me about Urquhart Castle and his plans for the mini-submarine.

"When I first met my husband, he was living in a camper on the edge of the Loch," she told me. "He started coming to my inn for meals. He had quit his job and left his fiancé to find the Loch Ness Monster."

"I see he hasn't given up his search."

"Not at all," she said. "And he finally got the attention of the BBC, of all things. I hope, for his sake, that they find something the next time he takes the sub down."

I watched the silver charm in the shape of a ship's anchor jingle from the rearview mirror. Sarah told me that the first summer they were married, he spent all his nights in a tent outside, so he could watch for the monster.

"That's how I know about the bagpipers," Sarah said. "He befriended them."

"Has it ever bothered you?" I asked. "His obsession?"

Sarah kept her eyes on the road. She wore a fuzzy sweater and corduroy pants. The inside of her car smelled like lavender. I worried I had pried too much, been too direct in my questioning.

"Some things you can get used to, and some things you can't," she said. "I've left men over much less, but, for whatever reason, I was willing to get used to this." She braked lightly as she negotiated the sharper curves in the road. "I think, one day, he'll find something that satisfies him and the quest will be over." She went quiet for a moment. "I'm not even sure what that would be like," she said. "What that would mean."

I looked out the window. Clouds, marbled with gray, loomed like mountains. I wondered what it was about me that Peter had decided he couldn't get used to. When we passed Urquhart Castle, the crumbling stone walls and fallen-in tower reminded me of a forgotten city.

I wandered through Reelig Glen, the dense vegetation brushing my knees, the shadows cast from the enormous

Douglas Firs darkening the ground. The twinflower had eluded me on this excursion, but I had collected samples of pilwort, a small fern. I'd only covered a portion of Reelig Glen and would continue my search tomorrow.

As I walked toward the edge of the glen—where I would meet Sam, who also worked at the Botany Institute—I started thinking of Peter and the night he told me he wanted to move out. He had stood at our living room window, tall and slack-shouldered, his tie loose around his neck. He had taken up with someone in Georgetown's zoology department, though, despite my repeated inquiries, he wouldn't tell me her name.

"I've learned something about myself in the last few years," he said. "I don't do well with repetition and routine."

"So you plan on going through the whole university, then?" I sat down and wedged a pillow between my knees. "For variety?"

"Emily," he said. "This would be a good time to start taking me seriously."

"What about our trip to Virginia Beach in February?" I felt my voice drop. "We'd talked about getting engaged."

"That was a mistake," he said. "I'm sorry, but it was."

I remained on the sofa, legs pulled to my chest, gaze averted. The spring semester had just ended. Out of professionalism, he explained, he had waited until the end of the term to leave. I wondered how long he'd been planning his exit, how long other people had known about the turn my life was going to take, while I carried on, oblivious to the way things were shifting beneath me like the tectonic plates before a quake. I remembered a time, during one of my childhood summers in the countryside, when my cousin fell into a well. I had been the one to hear the faint bleating of her voice, to find her crouched in the stone bottom of the well, wet and cold and in darkness—an image I would, in the days following Peter's announcement, be unable to shake.

That night, Peter left the apartment and didn't return until morning. I stayed on the sofa all night, my face blotched and puffy from crying. He moved out two days later. A week passed before I was able to pack away the little things he'd left behind—his wash cloth, a blue bowl, an empty picture frame, an encyclopedia, a miniature globe—and push the Tupperware box underneath the bed.

After Peter was settled in his Cleveland Park apartment, I called the director of the Botany Institute, who I'd met when she was a guest lecturer at Georgetown, and said I would be pleased to join the Inverness team over the summer. Before leaving Washington, I met Peter for a drink and he offered his new phone number.

"We'll keep in touch," he said, as though he had decided for both of us. "No reason to not be civil." And, because I wanted so badly to not lose him in a completely permanent way, I had taken down his number on a cocktail napkin without argument.

I stopped, pulled a notebook and pencil from my backpack, and sketched the tear-shaped leaves that clung to a tree trunk: quick gray lines across the graph paper, on which I had also charted the proximities of different plant species. I photographed and measured the vines, as I did with all the specimens, and then returned the supplies to my backpack and stepped out of the forest.

I left the shade of the trees and entered a long field, the grass tall and curved from a light wind. In the distance, I saw Sam standing at our agreed meeting place. Every afternoon, he took my samples to the lab and then drove me back to the Craigdarroch.

"Find anything good?" he asked when I reached him.

"Not much," I said. "Just a little pilwort for the lab."

As we walked to his car, he mentioned seeing the monster hunters on his way to Reelig Glen. "They were crossing the lake in a motorboat," he said. "One of them was looking at the water through some kind of telescope."

I asked if it was McKay, but Sam shrugged and said he had been too far away to tell.

"The chances of you finding a thousand twinflowers are better than their odds," he said. "If something is in that lake, I don't think it wants to be found."

"Maybe the twinflowers don't either," I said, eliciting a smile from Sam. When we reached the car, I glanced back once more at the dark thicket of trees and the shadows the shifting clouds had cast across the field.

After a dinner of oatcakes and salmon, which I took in my room, forgoing a meal with the monster hunters, I sat on the edge of my bed and dialed Peter's number. It was late afternoon in Washington; there was a chance he'd be home if he wasn't teaching a summer class or attending a meeting. I didn't leave a message when the machine came on, but hung up and dialed the number again. After two rings, a woman answered, her voice soft and unfamiliar. I heard the boom of a television in the background.

"Am I speaking to 32 Hilyer Point?" I asked.

"No," the woman said. "You're not speaking to a house."

"Is Peter around?"

She paused. "I don't think he can come to the phone now."

I sifted through the clatter of female voices from university parties and commencements, but couldn't place hers. Before I replied, the volume of the television increased and I caught an actor's familiar baritone; I recognized the voice from an old movie Peter liked, the one we periodically watched when there was nothing interesting in the theaters. I pictured him on the sofa, his long arms crossed behind his head.

"Are you watching *The French Connection*?" I asked the woman. "Has Hackman gotten to his 'never trust anyone' line yet?"

I stopped for a moment, pressed my fingertips against my cheek. The silence on the other end didn't break.

"When the line comes, you should remember it," I said. "It's one of Peter's favorites."

I heard whispers and static before the dial tone buzzed in my ear. I dropped the phone onto the mattress and checked the clock that hung over the dresser. I'd passed Ian in the hall after returning from Reelig Glen and he had extended a late night drink invitation. They would all be in the malt shop by now, expecting me. Before leaving, I wrapped a shawl embroidered with gold and brown flowers around my shoulders. I scrubbed my face and combed my hair, pushed my lips together and dotted them with red.

When I found the men in the malt shop, they were laughing loudly, apparently in response to a joke Theodore had told, though, despite Dale's urging, he would not repeat it. I asked where Sarah was, and McKay said she was balancing the books in her office, that she often worked late into the night. Sarah had left an open bottle of wine for me on the bar. I poured myself a glass and joined the men at their table, where we all toasted the Craigdarroch.

"One more day, and we'll be on our way home." Ian pushed his empty glass toward the center of the table and leaned back in his chair.

"If everything goes as planned at Urquhart," Dale said.

"We've been here for nearly two months. We've checked every inch of that lake, with military strength equipment for christsakes. There's nothing there. Just some trout and sturgeon." Theodore paused, looked at McKay. "And a few unusually large salmon."

"We haven't checked Urquhart Bay," McKay said. "We haven't gone to the bottom."

Theodore left the table to get another drink and, upon returning, drained the glass. "Come on, McKay," he said. "When are you going to shut up about the bottom?"

Dale and Ian looked uneasily together, then at me. Ian, seeming anxious to change the subject, asked how my work was coming along.

"It's going fine," I said. "The weather has been good for field work." I brushed my lips with the tip of my index finger, as if to make sure the color was still in place. I was unaccustomed to wearing lipstick; the tube of Ruby Rush in my room had been an impulse buy at the airport.

"What will be done with the specimens you've collected?" Dale asked.

"They'll be analyzed," I replied. "And we'll determine precisely what habitat the endangered plants require." The chemical analysis was Peter's specialty. Perhaps he was alone now, or maybe he and the woman had gone out for the evening. I took a long sip of wine and felt my face grow warm.

"I don't understand your work." Theodore didn't speak directly to me, but addressed the group, his voice rising. "Where's the science in preservation?" He leaned toward me, his chest nearly flat against the table. "Where's the advancement?"

The other men were silent. To avoid provoking Theodore, I told myself, staring into my half-empty wine glass. All my training and experience, the multitude of ways I could illustrate the importance of my work, in those tensely quiet moments, vanished from my mind. I could only think of Peter and how his evening might be unfolding. Had they finished the movie by now? Were they preparing to leave for a restaurant, Anna Maria's or Café Citron, or having a drink on the front steps of his new building? I couldn't let go of the idea that Peter was simply transferring the customs we once shared to this new person, that within a few months the woman would grow into the very space I once occupied, as though I had never been there at all.

When I looked up, all the men, even McKay, were tilting forward, wide-eyed. I finished my wine in two gulps, then pressed my lips together, certain that by now all the color had been transferred to the rim of the glass.

I pushed back my chair and stood. Ian rose and began to say something, but I turned from the table and left the malt shop. I stepped onto the porch, where I sat on a wood bench and gazed into the Loch. The bench was next to a window and I heard the men's voices, although I could not distinguish the words, only the alternately high and low pitches. I assumed they were talking about me.

The night was clearer than most and I was able to see stars, bunched together like handfuls of confetti. After nightfall, it was difficult to tell where the land disappeared into the water, but I could distinguish the boundaries of the Loch by the geography: perfectly smooth, a long sprawl of darkness.

I didn't hear McKay approaching the porch, and only realized he was there when I looked up and found him standing next to the bench. He wore a denim jacket, the fabric thin around the collar and elbows. He sat next to me, crossed his legs and rested his hands on his knees.

"You shouldn't listen to Theodore when he drinks," he said.

I shrugged. "I suppose preservation isn't the most exotic of the sciences."

"It's not so different from what I do," he said. "This is just a job for the others, but not for me. I've spent a lot of my life looking."

"Sarah told me about your search," I said. "She said you were living by the lake when she first met you."

McKay told me that one evening, many years ago, he saw the Loch Ness Monster footage Tim Dinsdale had shot in the sixties on a TV program. He said it was like a switch inside him was turned on, and he knew that the life he had been leading, the job at the IT firm and the fiancée, was over.

"After a month on the Loch, I ran out of food," he said. "The Craigdarroch was the closet place to go for meals. I'm embarrassed to say that several months passed before I even noticed Sarah."

"What finally got your attention?"

"She took me into her office one afternoon and showed me the photos that visitors to Loch Ness had taken of the monster over the years." She had framed them and hung them on the walls, a little something for the tourists. She had all the famous ones, the pictures taken by Hugh Gray and Robert Wilson and Frank Searle, but she had several others that he had never seen before, images that were vaguer, capturing only dark blotches or hazy shapes in the water—but, to McKay, no less exciting.

"That day in her office, she took down all the photos and gave them to me," McKay said. "She took them out of the frames one by one and put them in my hands. And I saw what I needed to see."

I was reminded of something from my graduate school days. It concerned one of the professors, Dr. Edgevale, who spent much of her career studying Sebastopol Meadowfoam, a rare species found in the forests of Northern California. I shared with McKay the story Dr. Edgevale told me one afternoon, in her office overlooking the campus quad. It was about the first time, after months of searching, she located a stand of Sebastopol Meadowfoam, how she had stood in the forest clearing for the longest time, staring at her discovery in disbelief; the stand she'd located sprawled on for several feet, the flowers bright white, the short stems plump as green slugs. How her world, in an instant, became as simple and small as petals and stems and rough-edged leaves.

"She said it was like looking at her life through a microscope," I told McKay. "The way everything blurred for a moment, then got sharp and distilled."

"I know just the feeling," he said.

"I wish I did," I said. "I really do."

We watched the Loch for a while. He mentioned this was one of the few summer nights he'd been able to see stars. Then McKay asked me if I knew about the first recorded sighting of the Loch Ness Monster. I shook my head.

"The first sighting was recorded in the manuscripts of St. Columba," he said. "Columba found a man who was being bitten to death by a water monster, and he made the sign of the cross, sending the creature away."

I crossed my arms; the shawl was draped across my thighs and waist, and I studied the arrangements of the gold and brown flowers as I listened to McKay continue, his voice papery and rhythmic.

"There was nothing for a while. Then a story was discovered in journals from the early 1800s. The author and two friends were boating in the southern part of the lake and suddenly a creature appeared and rushed the boat, sending huge sprays of water into the air. The man wrote that it looked as though the monster was coming through a tunnel of water." McKay spread his arms and raised his hands. "The swells overturned the boat and the man thought he and his friends were all most certainly dead. But, and this is the strangest part, the monster disappeared and in no time the lake was calm again and the men swam safely to shore."

"Are you frightened when you go down in the submarine?"

"You can't fear what you seek." He reached into his shirt pocket and pulled out a cigar. "Got a match?"

I had a matchbook in my pocket, for lighting the candles in my room. I struck a match and cupped my hand around the flame. As he leaned in, I recognized the musky smell of the cigar.

"Do you often walk around the Loch at night?"

"I go out after the bagpipers leave," he said. "We're not the first team to go on such an expedition, you know. Dozens of research teams have searched this lake and all of them came up empty. I like to see what might happen when nobody else is looking."

"Maybe there's nothing in the lake."

"Science is missing something." He stood, releasing a gray cloud from the corner of his mouth. "We're missing that thing I feel when I'm underwater."

"And what is that?"

"The feeling that the entire submarine could vanish at any moment."

"What does Sarah think of your theories?"

He smiled. "My wife is very patient."

"I wish I could say the same about the man who used to live with me," I said. "Although I'm not even sure what it was he grew impatient with."

"Well," he said, no longer smiling. "One could argue that Sarah's been more patient than she should have been."

I asked McKay what he had planned for tomorrow. He said they would be repairing one of the underwater cameras attached to the submarine.

"And the next morning?"

"We'll begin the descent at eight."

"I might walk down and watch," I said. "I've never seen a submarine in action before."

He took out his watch and dangled it in front of his face. The smoke around him had thickened, and I felt like I was speaking to him through a screen. I rose and brushed the creases from my slacks. "Going inside?"

"Not for a while," he said.

"Goodnight, then."

As I was leaving the porch, McKay asked if I had time for a short drive. He said there was something he wanted to show me.

"I've got nothing but time," I said.

He went into the inn to retrieve the van keys. When he returned, we departed for Urquhart Castle. There were no streetlights lining the road, and the sheen thrown from the car looked strange against the deep dark of the land. When we got to the castle, McKay pulled onto a gravely shoulder and parked.

"Did you bring a flashlight?" I asked once we were outside.

"Don't need one," he said. He wrapped his fingers around my elbow and guided me over a low wall and down a hill. As we walked, I looked all around; even the silhouette of the tower and the mountaintops were barely visible in the thick darkness. When we reached level ground, McKay stopped in front of a dark object and released my arm. He leaned toward the object and pulled off a covering. I heard something that sounded like a door opening and then a clicking noise. Two circular headlights beamed on. We were standing in front of the mini-submarine. The submarine rested on a box-shaped metal grate, and a white tarp was heaped on the ground. I touched the side of the vessel; the metal was cold. The top of the submarine had been opened.

"Go ahead," McKay said, helping me climb into the submarine. The interior was even smaller than I had imagined, barely enough room for me to turn my body. The control panel stretched out in front of me, the dials and compasses rimmed with green light, and there was a small black screen to the left of the panel. Cold air gusted through the open door. I looked up and saw the heavy black of the sky. In the distance, I heard the bagpipers.

"Close the door," I said to McKay. I listened to the creaking metal, the whoosh of air leaving the submarine. When the door was shut, I touched the rectangular window above the control panel. The glass was tinted, slick.

I knocked on the side of the submarine. The sound echoed around me. A few minutes passed before McKay knocked back. He said something, too, but his voice was muffled by the metal walls. I shouted that I couldn't hear him, and then the door sighed open and I felt the cold on my face. McKay hung over the opening, looking down at me. When I stared up at him, I noticed the gray swatches of hair at his temples, the little creases around his lips. Though he wasn't an old man, he looked, in the light that rose from the inside of the submarine, weary, a little wizened.

"Are you all right down there?" he asked.

"I could stay here for hours." I moved my hands over the control panel, the smooth faces of the dials. The moonlight shifted, and the metal interior suddenly gleamed silver. I asked him about the screen to the left of the control panel, and he said it was a sonar, used to track the underwater sounds. He said it could indicate how close the noise was and where it was originating from.

"I've been trying to get Sarah in here for weeks," he said. "I've always wanted her to know immersion."

"It must be like another world down there," I said, pointing at the water ahead. "Underneath the Loch."

Being down in the submarine made me feel calmer, less restless. I forgot about the earlier unpleasantness with Theodore, and I did not think of Peter until long after we had left Urquhart Castle. When McKay reached into the submarine and extended his hand, I was reluctant to take it.

25

I was not prepared for the storm. Excited from the trip to Urquhart Castle, I'd gone to bed late the night before and, annoyed with myself for getting a slow start, I'd rushed out of the Craigdarroch without a raincoat. A heavy spurt soaked my long-sleeved cotton shirt; water dripped from my ponytail and strands of hair stuck to the side of my face. By the afternoon, the sun had broken through and the rain had lightened, although water still fell, cold against my cheeks and white-knuckled hands.

The geography of Reelig Glen turned greener and shadier as I trekked further into the forest, mirroring the leafy and shadowed habitat the twinflower preferred. There had been several false alarms—two flowers growing close together that, from a distance, resembled the double bell of the *Linnaea borealis*. As I stepped carefully through the wet grass, the straps of my backpack digging into my shoulders, I wondered what, if anything, McKay had told the other men or Sarah about our outing last night.

At first, I thought the flower ahead was another false alarm. It was too slight to be a twinflower and the color was different. But as I drew closer, I saw the unmistakable bell-shaped blossoms sagging underneath the weight of the rainwater. The blooms were wilted and the color was lighter than it should have been, almost white. It seemed to be leaning forward, as though the roots were separating from the soil and the entire flower was in danger of collapsing. It looked nothing like the twinflowers I'd seen in photographs and slide shows, and I was absent of the feelings Dr. Edgevale had described: the exhilaration, the sense of purpose.

I tucked the wet strands of hair behind my ears and set off to find another twinflower, walking several miles. As I searched the woods, I thought of the calendar I once purchased at a gardening shop in Dupont Circle and kept tacked to the corkboard in our kitchen. Poppies in May. Snapdragons in August. Columbines in November. Moth and ghost orchids marked the gray and icy winter months. And then, in April, the twinflower: two bright pink bells affixed to a sturdy green stem growing from a smooth mound of black soil. I remembered the entries for that month so clearly, reminders for faculty meetings and dinners and theater tickets printed in black ink—the evidence of a life that no longer belonged to me.

I continued the hunt until daylight slipped away and darkness, which seemed to rise from the forest floor, took over. Only then did I return to the twinflower. I unzipped my backpack, pulled out a flashlight, and aimed it at the ground. As I watched the blossoms struggle to sustain the blows of the large raindrops falling from the tree branches above, it seemed not even the most vigorous preservation effort could coax such a delicate species through the centuries to come. Still, it wasn't until I reached for the flower, with the intention of placing it in a plastic specimen bag, that the wave rolled over me, that I realized I could continue looking for the brilliant specimen I'd envisioned, could still have everything Dr. Edgevale had described.

I left Reelig Glen that day without collecting any data from the twinflower. When I met Sam—he caught my attention by waving two flashlights, the beams, for a moment, resembling large yellow eyes—on the outskirts of the glen, I told him I had been unable to locate a twinflower. And later, when another member of the research team discovered the very twinflower I had abandoned, I acted shocked and said I hadn't been able to see very well through the rain and night.

The bagpipers did not play that evening because of the weather. The ground floor of the inn was quiet, as the other scientists had declined another night at the malt shop, completing final equipment repairs and packing instead. After returning from Reelig Glen, I had wandered around the Craigdarroch, hoping to bump into Sarah or McKay, or perhaps to even see them together, to witness some private moment of their marriage, but no one was around.

Later in the evening, I sat at the desk in my bedroom and stared out the window. I had discovered in the desk drawer a thin stack of Craigdarroch stationery, envelopes, and a black pen with the hotel name embossed along the side in gold. I placed a sheet of paper on the desk and picked up the pen and began to write.

July 20th
Inverness, Scotland

Peter:

Today it rained. Today I found a twinflower. It was, like so many other things, not at all what I had hoped. But it is a flower and only a flower and how could I have grown to expect so much from it? Perhaps this is the origin of disappointment. When we give something more power than it could ever possibly possess.

How is it that you are already leading a different life?

I cannot say that I wish you well. Maybe one day I will.

E

I sealed the letter in an envelope and returned it to the drawer. I planned to send it the next afternoon, after I had returned from watching McKay's descent into the Loch, not yet knowing that I would forget the letter altogether until

I had left Inverness and was flying back to Washington, that I wouldn't speak of it until I saw Peter at a botany convention in Chicago a year later, where I would press my legal pad against my chest and say, After we parted, I wrote you a letter, but I left it in a desk in Scotland.

I folded my arms on the desktop and rested my head against them. I listened to the rain beat the roof and watched it coat the glass—the panes looked like they were melting—until it eased and the night turned still. There was a knock at the door. It was Sarah, coming to deliver me a bowl of soup and some bread, which was wrapped in a paper towel. I thanked her and set the tray down on my desk.

"I wanted to make sure you got a proper dinner," she said.

"You've been very kind," I said. "You and your husband both."

"I heard he took you to Urquhart Castle last night." Her hair was pulled back, and she wore thin gold bracelets on her wrists. "That's where he'll depart from tomorrow morning."

"For the last time," I said. "Unless they find something, of course."

"The last time for now," she said.

I sat in the chair. "Does it worry you when he goes down in the submarine?"

"I've gotten used to that too." She looked down at the floor for a moment. "One afternoon, last summer, McKay went diving with an underwater camera. Did he tell you about this already?"

I shook my head. Sarah told me that she had been in the lobby when he came running into the Craigdarroch, still in his wetsuit, wild with excitement. He said he'd seen the Loch Ness Monster, that he'd captured the creature on tape, that he finally had proof. He called two marine biologists he knew at the University of Aberdeen and they drove up to Inverness the next morning.

"While we waited for these men, he told me what the monster looked like," Sarah said. "He said its fins resembled gossamer, that the color of its skin was deep green, like peat moss." But, she continued, when the biologists arrived and watched the tape, there was nothing to see, just footage of lake water. McKay had protested, said something must have gone wrong with the recording, but they didn't believe him and left.

"He doesn't think I believed him either," she said. "He's still angry about it."

"Did you believe him?"

"I wanted to."

"And there was really nothing on the tape?"

"Not a thing," she said. "I watched it several times by myself, pausing and rewinding, looking for just the smallest sign."

She sighed and pushed up her sweater sleeves. She apologized for taking so much of my time, said I must be anxious to get some rest. We wished each other goodnight. After she left, I stood by the closed door and listened to her footsteps going down the stairs.

I woke early the next morning and set out for Urquhart Castle. The sun was rising when I started down the road; the landscape seemed so different than the one McKay and I had passed in the night. Gold light crept through the fog that was draped across the mountains, and the treetops poked through the haze like spears.

Once I reached the ruins, I stopped beside the tower and looked over the stone wall. The men stood on the bank, holding radios and backpacks full of equipment; the mini-submarine was already floating in the shallow waters of the lake. I wandered around the ruins, the hunks of stone, the slanted tower. I climbed the chipped steps, stood at the top of the structure, and gazed into the Loch. The surface of the lake was rippled like silk.

McKay waded into the water and climbed inside the submarine. Then Ian slapped the metal top and the men pushed the submarine into deeper waters. I noticed a figure sitting on the grassy hill between the castle and the water's edge. It was Sarah, watching her husband's descent with a pair of small binoculars. She sat with her elbows resting on her knees, the binoculars wedged between her pale hands. I wondered how many times she'd watched McKay disappear into the Loch, how many more times she would watch him before her patience ran out. There was unhappiness, I could tell, and yet I longed to know what held them together, as though that could give me some sense of how to set about repairing my own life.

The submarine disappeared gradually, like a vessel that had sprung a slow leak. I wondered what McKay was seeing through that tinted window. Murky water, shimmering fish darting past? The wind increased and it looked as though the breezes might lift the water like a dark curtain. Ian, Theodore, and Dale spread across the bank, occasionally speaking into their radios. Sarah was as still as a sentinel, and I wondered if this was an accurate portrait of their life together: he goes, she waits. I watched until the small waves closed over the dome of the submarine like a mouth. I had three more weeks in Inverness, and I imagined the days stretching before me like the clean gray lines of my graph paper.

I went down the tower steps and over the stone wall, moving toward Sarah. Fog was nestled in the crevices of hills, as though the clouds were unraveling. A gust of wind blew my hair across my face; strands stuck to my lips. When I reached Sarah, I sat next to her and pressed my palms into the grass.

"I'll wait with you," I said.

Without lowering the binoculars, Sarah asked what it was like being down in the submarine. "The other scientists brought it with them from London," she said. "McKay's been after me to sit inside it, but I didn't want to."

I told her about the control panel and the window above it, about the sonar screen and the creaking noise the door made when it closed. "It seems like a lonely place to spend so much time."

"Lonely," she repeated, placing the binoculars in her lap. "That's one thing my husband's never been afraid of."

I leaned back on my hands. "So now we just watch the Loch?"

She wiped her cheek with the sleeve of her sweater. "Doesn't it just look like the kind of thing that could swallow a person up?"

"If he really does see something, I hope the recording equipment works."

"Oh, god." She rested a hand against her forehead. "Me too."

We were quiet for a while. The sun had fully risen, turning the sky into a clear expanse of blue. Sarah passed the binoculars to me, then lay on her back and closed her eyes. Her hair fanned around her head; the light hit the elegant line of her cheekbones. I wished McKay was here to witness her beauty.

I raised the binoculars to my eyes. Up close, the water was choppier, dappled with light. I scanned the Loch, but I didn't see any sign of the submarine preparing to break through the surface and rise into the open air. I thought back to the night McKay took me to Urquhart Castle. What I had told Sarah, I realized, was not actually true; the submarine hadn't struck me as a lonely place to be. It was removed, it was its own dimension, and that was what I had liked about being down there—that the whole mess of my life had felt so very far away. I wondered if this same feeling was what kept drawing McKay underwater, if that was, perhaps, the essence of what he and Sarah had been arguing about the morning I interrupted them. I was making things up now, I understood. For all I knew, I could have gotten it all wrong.

I increased the focus on the binoculars, wishing it was possible to see beneath the surface and all the way to the bottom of the Loch. I imagined it was me, not McKay, that was moving through the water in the submarine, the headlights piercing shadows, the interiors of caves. I imagined seeing the lines on the sonar screen shoot up and down, and then discovering the sound wasn't originating from a particular place, but coming from everywhere, all at once. I imagined the sound passing through the walls of the submarine, a great hum that made the metal shudder, as though the vessel was being shaken like a toy. When a dark something moved in front of the window, the object was too large to identify; I only saw pieces and parts of a giant mass. And it was not fear that I felt, but a wanting. You can't fear what you seek, McKay had told me on the porch, and I would want to know what the world held. That was one thing I felt sure of. I put down the binoculars and looked at Sarah. Her eyes were still closed. I shut mine, joining her in that darkness.

the rain season

From the only window in my concrete one-room house, I watch a woman drag a pointed stick through the black dirt. I know what she is drawing—the same thing the villagers have been sketching in the ground for the past week, when rumors of disappearances in the forest began to spread. In the mornings, I go out to buy fish and yams and step over their creations: creatures shaped like elephants or hippopotamuses with long tails and claws. Sometimes a horn juts out of the forehead, sometimes not. The month is May, the peak of the rain season. Every afternoon, water rushes over the drawings. Still the woman outside continues, kneeling and hunched, opening the earth with the tip of her stick. She is drawing a legend.

There are only two seasons in the Congo: the dry season and the wet season. The heat is constant, the humidity unrelenting. I never slept naked before coming here, not even with my husband, but now I undress every night before burrowing underneath the white sheets. I sleep little and when I do, I dream of ash, gray mountains that collapse into rivers and flood the streets and seep underneath my door, filling my house with a dark fog. I am sure this has something to do with the fire.

The parish sent me to Africa in December. Father Hughes was reluctant at first, as I had no prior missionary experience and rarely attended Mass with my husband, but, as it would turn out, he was unable to enlist another volunteer for this part of the world. I taught children English and basic arithmetic until the school closed two weeks ago because of the riots and fighting. Elections are approaching, rebel groups wrestling for power. In a recent demonstration, a UN worker and two civilians were killed. I have not been in touch with Father Hughes, despite his requests for updates. I do not know how much longer the parish will continue to send money.

The woman rises, her knees caked with dirt. She strides away, gripping the stick like a spear, her arm flexed as though she's preparing to hurl it into the distance. When she's gone, I go outside and examine the drawing, my shadow long and flat against the ground. Her creature is larger than the other renderings I've seen, although it lacks the horn. The villagers call it mokele-mbembe, or "one who stops the flow of rivers." Drawing the monster is supposed to keep it from leaving Lake Tele, which lies several miles beyond the lush perimeter of the jungle.

Expeditions to Lake Tele have unearthed little in the way of evidence. Many years ago, a biologist and an animal trader discovered massive footprints and broad paths of flattened grass. They even photographed mokele-mbembe emerging from the lake, or so the story goes. But after leaving the forest, they boarded a train bound for the southern part of the region and there was an accident. The biologist and animal trader were killed when their car overturned, and the camera was destroyed. The other passengers survived. The cause of the crash was never determined. This is the story the locals tell me when I ask questions about the monster.

I crouch in the dirt and use my index finger to draw a horn just above the snout. I am several feet away from the edge of the jungle; the border is vivid green and heavy with vines and leaves. I reach into my pocket and feel my husband's coin, round and slick, a smooth silver circle. He brought it back from Spain, where, in his youth, he taught English at an American School. He found it on the floor of the Segovia Cathedral and considered it a sign of good fortune.

The air thickens, a hot wind blows through. I look up at the low, swollen clouds. As I stand and start towards the house, fat raindrops splatter against my arms and fill the indentations in the earth, rubbing away the image.

In the evening, after the rain eases, Oji visits. The knock on my door startles me. While eating dinner, boiled yams straight from the pot, I heard a faraway blast of gunfire. I dropped the spoon and pushed away the pot, stood at the window and tugged on my ponytail. My hair, once thick and long, is thinning; pale strands cling to the shoulders of my shirt.

I find Oji leaning against the wall, dressed in torn khaki shorts and a faded red T-shirt, water dripping from his earlobes and chin. After inviting him inside, I get a towel from the bathroom and mop his face and wiry hair. He is twelve years old, a student of mine. He lives on the outskirts of the village, in the scattering of houses beyond the school and the markets. Both his parents are ill, far beyond recovery.

"Catherine," he says. "You wear it."

I pinch the tiny, carved bird hanging from my neck. Oji gave me the necklace after a demonstration in the village square. The carving has been blessed by his grandfather, a medicine man. It is supposed to keep me safe.

"Yes," I say. "I wear it always."

He holds a guava to his chest. I offer my palm and he hands it to me.

"Shall we cut it?"

He nods.

I take a knife from the drawer and press the guava against the counter; juice oozes from the split skin. I cut his half into slivers and push them aside. He eats his portion in two wet bites.

"My uncle said mokele-mbembe killed a farmer yesterday and drug him into the forest."

"I thought mokele-mbembe was an herbivore." I turn on the faucet and rinse my hands in the sink.

He wipes his mouth on the back of his hand. "Same as a dinosaur?"

Some believe the creature is a sauropod dinosaur, a survivor from the pre-historic age. I read a description of the monster in a book once: inky eyes, skin the color of rust, a body thick with muscle and scales. "No." I turn off the water and dry my hands on my jeans. "It means an animal that only eats plants."

He circles the room, stopping at the foot of my bed and staring at the empty space over the headboard, his feet near a metal pan where water has been collecting from a leak in the roof. He points to the nail sticking out of the wall. "Where did it go?"

A clay cross, the color of a sunset, used to hang over the bed. Father Hughes gave it to me before I left for Africa. Send pictures, he said, folding my hand around the cross. He told me the congregation would want to track my progress. Seeing the cross above my bed always reminded me of my husband's stories from Catholic school, the prayers he recited, his scapular and rosary, the crucifixes that hung at the front of every classroom.

"I took it down. I was worried it was going to fall on my head while I was sleeping." At first, I blamed the images of smoke and ash that kept invading my sleep on my proximity to the cross, an emblem of how a life of goodness failed my husband. A few days ago, I loaded pamphlets from the parish, a stack of bibles, and the cross into a box and pushed it into a corner, but my dreams were unchanged.

His mouth droops. "I liked the color."

I squeeze his shoulder; his skin is still damp. Once I saw his mother waiting for him outside the school, emaciated and wet-eyed, purple and red lesions molting across her forehead. It was the last time she left the house,

Oji says when I ask how she's doing. His father is even farther along, barely able to raise a hand from the bed. My husband and I never had children, never thought we were suited for it, so I am surprised to find myself enjoying having a child in my care. Sometimes we do arithmetic or reading lessons when he visits, or he tells me stories about the jungle. I worry about what would happen to him if I were to leave.

"I'll look for another cross the next time I go to the market."

He grins, his teeth small and white. "Like the one you had?"

I nod, surprised he prefers the rough, orange-red surface of the cross to something bright and glazed. I look outside; the rain has stopped and dusk is drawing color from the sky.

I take three potatoes from the glass jar sitting on the counter and drop them into a paper bag. Every week I fill the jar with potatoes and yams, but lately there has been less food at the market; some of the farmers have joined the rebels and others are frightened to be near the forest, where their crops grow. I pass Oji the bag. "Go before it gets dark."

He nods and clutches the neck of the sack. He thanks me, asks me to visit him soon. I promise that I will. After the school closed and a rebel group vandalized a government building in a nearby town, Susannah, a missionary I taught with, came to my house. She had arranged to fly back to California and urged me to contact the US Embassy, to return to my home in Chicago. I don't know what you've left, but it can't be worse than what's coming here, she said, handing me a slip of paper with her phone number. Last week, I bought a plane ticket and the flight is three days away and I still don't know if I want to take it. From the window, I watch Oji leave, cradling the bag in his arms, his small footprints lingering in the wet dirt.

I wake from a dream curled and hugging my knees, my body slippery with sweat. I hear a dull roar, as though a seashell is pressed against my ear. Even before the fire, I had apocalyptic dreams. Collapsing bridges, falling buildings— all a precursor, I now believe, to the disaster preparing to overtake my life. I would describe them to my husband in the mornings, standing behind him in the bathroom while he shaved. Silly girl, he would say before tapping his razor against the side of the sink and rinsing his face. We met at Northwestern, and we were married for eleven years. The friends from college that I kept in touch with would, later in their marriages, complain about their husbands changing: he used to like going to movies on weekends, but now he spends Saturdays at the office or he painted my walls when we were dating, but now I can't get him to take out the trash or he used to tell me everything, but now he acts like our conversations are causing him pain. My husband, however, stayed exactly the same, as though his traits were fossilized: practical, ingenious with crossword puzzles, bad at small talk, stubborn, quietly devout, capable of being both surprisingly pitiless and surprisingly kind. In all our years together, he was never frightened by his dreams, which was how I knew he kept believing in God.

Susannah's number is in the woven basket I keep next to the bed. I take out the slip of paper and go to the phone affixed to the wall; the black cord is frayed and dangling. The dial tone ripples with static. It's late afternoon in California. I call the number.

"I've been seeing the news," Susannah says after she answers. "Everything is going crazy."

"It's nothing prayers can help." Before the mail service was disrupted, the cheerful postcards from friends and relatives turned into worried letters about when I would be coming home. Last week, I gathered the letters and burned them in a garbage can behind my house. I ask Susannah what it's like to be back in California.

"Strange at first," she says. "The heat is different. Lighter." When she starts talking about her husband's ballpoint pen company and making pies for church potlucks, her words grow thick with static and I lose my way in the growl of her voice. I realize I can't follow regular conversations anymore, as though the life Susannah describes is now as foreign to me as monsoons and jungles and legends of monsters once were.

The line goes quiet and she asks if I'm all right.

"Listen," I tell her. "I might not take that flight. I'm thinking of changing my ticket, of staying a little longer."

"Catherine." The line clears momentarily and her voice rings through my body like a bell. "There is no 'later.' There is only leaving now, or not at all."

I tell her about the schoolchildren. I see them roaming the streets, restless and unmoored as boats in a storm, or crouched beneath the overhangs of buildings, playing with half-deflated bicycle tires. I see their parents, so many of them sick or preparing to fight. I repeat the stories I've heard about people in other villages who fled and, so they could move faster, left behind their youngest children to be killed or forced to carry guns for the enemy.

"We've done all we can for them," she says. "You're not going to change anything by staying."

I tell her that I can't explain it, but I feel like I belong here, and then the line bursts with static and goes dead.

I reach underneath the bed, drag out a small radio, and turn it on. *The Department of State warns U.S. Citizens against travel. Fighting continues in Brazzaville, Kinshasa, and Liranga. The plan to implement national elections raises the possibility of civil disturbance. Unofficial armed groups known to—*

I click off the radio. It's raining again; water hammers the tin roof. Last year, summer rains submerged crops and uprooted houses. I heard stories of villagers wading through waist-deep water, of drowned animals and fallen trees.

A heat wave washed over Chicago last summer. The temperature hovered at one hundred degrees for days, train rails warped, the water levels in the lakes dropped, the city opened cooling centers. I tried staying inside and working on my latest batch of freelance articles—on everything from growing pepper plants on apartment balconies for *The Urban Gardener* to outdoor jazz concerts in Grant Park for *The Chicago Traveler*—but it was too hot to concentrate. When our air conditioner gave out, my husband and I found our own shadowed corners in the house, and it felt like I went days without hearing his voice. One night we fought, the same sort of argument that rose from the insurmountable differences in our own natures, to which there was never a solution. In bed, he turned from me and fell asleep quickly. I stared out the window for a while, at the moonlight shifting on the scorched lawn, then went downstairs to watch television.

I fell asleep on the couch, to the drone of a reporter talking about the latest in heat-related deaths, and woke with smoke in my lungs. The haze was so thick, I couldn't see the four walls of the room; I heard the cracking of flames. Before I realized I was moving forward, I was running out of the house, into the driveway, to the neighbor next door. Running in a cotton nightgown that fell to my knees, coughing furiously, the asphalt blurring and glistening under the streetlights. After seeing the thick curls of smoke unfurling in the air, the neighbor called the fire department. I went back and circled the house, shouting for my husband when I saw smoke billowing from an upstairs window. I pushed the front door open and stumbled into the hallway; smoke had spread across the ceiling like a thundercloud. I heard footsteps behind me and knocked into two firemen; they draped a blanket over my shoulders and pulled me into the street. I remember the wail of the trucks and water disappearing into huge orange plumes, an oxygen mask against my face and the bloody soles of my feet.

The house melted into a heap of charred beams. I later learned the fire was electrical, caused by an overloaded circuit in our study. Earlier in the summer, my husband complained about an outlet sparking when he plugged in his computer. I suggested having someone check the outlets, but neither of us ever got around to making the call. After the funeral, I went to a motel. Family—my sister-in-law in Wyoming, my aunt and cousins on the East Coast, my brother and his Canadian wife in Montreal—and friends called and left sympathy cards at the front desk after I told the manager I didn't want to be disturbed. Their messages were the same, all so painfully insufficient. *You're always welcome at our house for dinner* and *I can't imagine what it's like to be you right now* and *At least you're still young and it's not too late to start over.* I unplugged the phone and closed the blinds. I listened to the noises seeping from other rooms. The boom of televisions. Arguments. The slamming of doors. Fucking. After a few nights, the sounds converged into a constant, lonely hum. I took long baths, sometimes staying in the tub after I had drained the water, time slipping forward, into the late night, without my awareness. I thought endlessly about what might have happened if I'd only thought, only been awake enough, to shout my husband's name up the stairs before running from the house, wondering, if God really existed, why he didn't reach into my chest and force the words out.

I tried going to Mass because I thought my husband would have wanted me to, but the prayers and the singing made the hollow feeling inside me worse, and the incense reminded me of the smoke that had consumed our house. During the Lord's Prayer, I didn't kneel, just sat upright in the pew, my hands flat against my thighs. After the service, I went to see Father Hughes, whom my husband had liked, and noticed the call for missionaries posted on the parish bulletin board, wedged between flyers for youth groups and daycare. I tore the flyer from the board and walked into Father Hughes's office. Send me, I said, waving the paper. He shook his head and took the flyer from me; he said I would be going for the wrong reasons, not because I had something to give, but because I had nothing left. And then, two weeks later, I got a call from Father Hughes and within a month, I was boarding a plane for Africa. When I walked into the heavy air for the first time, I knew I'd found a place as strange as the world I'd come to occupy in my mind.

Before leaving for Africa, I hired a crew to clear the debris. When I went to the lot to pay the workers, they gave me a shoebox. I opened it after they left and found— amongst brass cabinet knobs, a silver cuff link, and a small copper dish—the coin my husband kept in his desk drawer, a shield engraved on one side, a lion's head on the other. It was the one he found in Spain, on the mosaic floor of a cathedral, the lion's head facing the stained glass sky. I sat on the curb, facing away from the flat, black square in the center of the yard, and watched cars pass on the street. After a while, I put the coin in my pocket and left the box sitting on the lawn.

The low-hanging Iroko tree branches scrape the roof. I dress, pausing to reach into the basket and feel the rough bottom until my fingers touch the coin. Outside the rain is light but steady. Water has pooled around my doorway. The roads are turning to mud. There are no streetlights. I cannot see the stars or moon. The darkness is vast.

I stop walking when I reach out and my hand brushes against bark and vines, thick and firm like the body of a snake. I think about what this jungle might be like in another month and promise myself to begin packing in the morning. I want to remember the quiet of this place, the unbroken darkness. Through the branches, I can't see anything beyond the rows of trees. I step inside the forest and listen.

I hear nothing but rain. I walk until I can no longer see the silhouette of my house when I glance over my shoulder. Snakes, hippopotamuses, and crocodiles live in the forest. And, if you believe the legend, mokele-mbembe. The villagers say the monster is noiseless, that it never roars or groans, that when it moves through the forest, the sound of branches being snapped or water parted fails to echo. If nothing else, I believe this. The worst things in life stalk in silence.

I hear a rustling, followed by a chirp, and look up, at the dark form that has landed on a branch. From the rounded shape and short wing span, it's probably a tinkerbird or a mousebird, although I can't be certain without seeing the color. When I first came to the village, I found a book, *Birds of the Congo*, at a market. The cover was creased and faded; some pages had been torn out or folded down, different types of birds circled in green ink. As I stepped away from the crowd and opened the book, I wondered where it came from and who left it behind. From my reading, I learned over two hundred and fifty species of birds exist in the Congo, and government officials estimate eighty percent of the lakes and forests in the region are unexplored.

The bird reminds me of the afternoon in February we took the schoolchildren on a field trip to Brazzaville to see the Basilique Sainte-Anne and the Municipal Gardens, where small green birds perched on the tree branches. Before we climbed back into the vans that would carry us home, we let the children play tag in a square outside the gardens. I stood apart from the other teachers and watched the students run in ziz-zags, ducking and lunging, the girls shrieking whenever one of them was tagged. Oji was the fastest. He might have won the game if he hadn't fallen and cut his knee. I sat with him on a bench, pressing a Kleenex against his wound, until it was time to leave. After we returned to our village, I offered to walk him home. It was then he told me the first story about mokele-mbembe. He said an American scientist and his assistant were paddling up the Congo River when the boat shuddered and a giant lizard-shaped head emerged. The monster craned its neck and stared at the men, then plunged back into the water. After the creature vanished, the river began to bubble and waves knocked the boat onto the bank. The men fled Africa and told other explorers to stay away from the Congo. When we reached his house, we went around the back and he showed me his drawings in the dirt, surrounded by sisal plants and flat, white rocks. He makes a new drawing at every dawn and dusk, some underneath the pointed sisal leaves, so they won't be washed away by the daily rains.

A twig snaps as I turn and move toward the road. Winds press against my back, guiding me out of the trees. My heart, my breath, is quiet. I am beyond fear, beyond any recognizable emotion, as though all my chest contains is a bundle of short-circuited wires. I'm only thirty-three and yet I feel like I've been walking the earth for hundreds of years. While crossing the street, I step in puddles that swallow my feet and ankles. The rain has slowed, but I still cannot see stars or the moon. Everything resembles a shadow.

My hair is damp when I boil water for tea in the morning. I run a hand through it and lose several strands. The creases in my hands are lined with dirt. I scrub them, but the black veins in my knuckles remain. I start packing, loading the bibles and church pamphlets into my duffel bag, then stop when I realize I'm only taking the things I would want to leave behind. On the radio, I listen to a report on the riot that has broken out in Kinshasa. Two police officers have been killed, stores and homes looted. Today I am going to the market.

I dress in a white shirt and tan pants, a belt pulled tight around my waist. I slip on sandals, knot my hair into a ponytail, and tie the carved bird around my neck. The string that it dangles from is weakening. Outside the air is damp and heavy, the sky edged with gray. I carry the bibles and the church pamphlets behind my house, and dump them into the same garbage can I used to burn the letters. I don't burn these, though; the can is too wet and I'm out of matches. I just look down at them, at the soot smeared across the white pamphlet paper. I imagine them getting soaked by rains; I imagine leaving them to rot.

Beyond my house, images of mokele-mbembe are already scattered across the ground, the lines wavy and imprecise in the wet earth. I see five drawings on my way to the market. The village center is quiet. The school is empty, the windows boarded with planks to deter looters. I don't stop to stare at the shuttered school, to touch the covered windows. The day Susannah came to see me, I nodded solemnly as she spoke, but her voice moved over me like a wave, her words somehow never hitting my ears, as though she was speaking to me through a thick sheet of glass. Who are we helping? she said, pointing out that we hadn't even seen most of the children since the school closed. We were standing outside; the sun was so bright, the sky looked ablaze. I wondered about my burned house, if the last of the ash had finally been carried away by rain and new growth. I didn't see how I could stay in the Congo much longer. The violence was increasing; the parish would eventually stop sending money. And yet I couldn't imagine leaving, couldn't imagine looking outside and not seeing the sprawl of green, not feeling the weight of the air.

I buy three yams from the produce stall, then wander through the cluster of stands, shaded by umbrellas that cast circular shadows. A man is selling dugout canoes carved from the tropical trees that grow in the forest. Another stall offers banana stalks and posho, a paste made from ground corn meal and sweet potatoes. People speak in various dialects, their words quick and sharp. I smell spices and sweat and rotten eggs. Two boys pass on bicycles, nearly brushing against me. The fish stall is closed, the owner's stool knocked to the ground. I ask a woman carrying a sack of peanuts, and she says he left to join the protestors in Kinshasa.

I stop at a stall that sells clay ornaments and carved animals. I run my fingertips over wooden elephants, glazed tigers, their mouths agape, and stacks of clay bowls. The owner asks if I want to buy something, but I shake my head and begin walking toward the outskirts of the village, the plastic bag filled with yams bumping against my leg.

I navigate around two young girls squatting and drawing mokele-mbembe with strips of metal, their dark hair braided. The sky is flat and purple. I hear thunder. Oji's house is in worse condition than the last time I saw it—white paint peeling, walls leaning inwards, tarnished window panes.

I stop when I see a man backing out of the house, gripping a pair of ankles. Another man emerges, holding elbows. The face is covered with a black sheet, but I can tell it's a woman's body from the length of the hair, which grazes the ground. Her hands are limp, her wrists thin as wire. Oji stands in the doorway. I am too far away to see if he is crying. The men carrying his mother are probably his uncles. I wonder where she will be buried. They load the body into the backseat of a truck and drive away, the taillights red smudges in the distance. Oji shouts and chases after them, momentarily disappearing from sight.

He returns with his head bowed, his arms twisted around his ribcage.

In the Congo, the dead are buried quickly, to keep them from returning as traveling ghosts. Later, carved masks will be placed by the grave, but her name will not be spoken again. The villagers fear the dead, blame them for nightmares and droughts, pray to them for healthy crops and solace.

I drop the bag of produce and run toward Oji. I call his name. He turns, stares at me for a moment, then reaches for my hand. We sit in the dirt. I have no words to offer, like my silence after the fire when friends and relatives called with their condolences, for what is a condolence but an attempt to bridge the unbridgeable. I cup my hand around the point of his shoulder. I wait for him to speak.

"Mokele-mbembe left the forest last night. My uncle found footprints close to his house," he finally says, spreading his fingers. "They were the size of an elephant's." A misty rain falls for several minutes, then passes. Oji suddenly appears older, the tightness in his jaw and the heaviness of his gaze. He grinds the base of his palm into the soil.

"Does it rain in America?" he asks. "Where you are from?"

"Sometimes."

"What did you leave there?"

"Not much," I reply. "I was married once." The night after the fire, I went back to the house and walked through the ash and burned wood and unidentifiable metal shapes. The heat wave had started to pass and the air was thin.

"Did you like each other?"

"Yes, we did. Sometimes we did." I remember the way the ash spread, across my hands and face and clothing; back in the motel, I rinsed it from my hair. I searched for something I could identify, something we had used or loved, but it all looked as though it had come from another world.

"My parents did not," he says. "Not really."

I take Oji's fist and uncurl his fingers, concentrating on the shapes of his knuckles. I reach into my pocket and place my husband's coin on his palm.

"For you," I say.

He rubs his thumb against the silver lion's head. "Where is it from?"

"From far away. A place I've never been." I tell Oji about my husband finding the coin on the floor of a holy place, that the coin traveled through many people to reach him. I tell him the coin holds secrets, pieces of lives.

Oji drops the coin into the square pocket on his T-shirt and flattens a hand against his chest. I've lost the desire to hold onto that last physical artifact of the life I once had, as though I was buried and re-emerged as a person who doesn't believe in anything except the way existence rages on, furiously unconscious of when one life ends and another begins. Lightning cracks across the sky and the rain begins, slanted by winds. I tilt my head back; the falling drops resemble millions of clear marbles.

"Go inside," I tell him. "Bad weather is coming."

He grabs my arm and holds on for a moment, his hand sliding from my wrist to my fingers. It's the first touch I've felt since my husband died that caused a pulse of feeling in my chest, the last spark of a live wire before it goes dead. Oji squeezes my fingertips, then lets go. He stands and walks to the house, pausing by the door and touching his chest before going inside.

I rise and find shelter underneath a broad canopy of umbrella tree leaves. I watch several of Oji's drawings blur into smooth patches of mud. The dirt surrounding the knotted roots is dry. I kneel and pick up an oval rock, the tip worn to a dull point. I push the rock into the ground and begin shaping the earth. I draw my monster with a great sharpened horn and peaked flames flowing from its mouth.

Lately I've been thinking of winter in Chicago. I can no longer remember the exact color of the snow—pure white or flecked with gray? I can only recall my husband and me moving inside a warm, low-lit house—the details of the house are gone from me too; I see a maze of bare walls and smooth floors that glow a pale blue—and the hushed sound of snow falling and banking along the sidewalk.

When I'm finished, I bend my fingers and look at my hands; my nails are packed with soil. The rain intensifies. Oji's house becomes vague, a long shadow. Winds shake the leaves and for a moment I smell smoke. I concentrate on the scent, but it vanishes into the aroma of rain and tree bark, the way one life can collapse into another and different people can stir within the same body, like bats thrashing inside a secret hollow.

up high in the air

J ust after the Fourth of July, my mother called to tell me she thought her hair was on fire. She lived in Nebraska, alone since my father drowned in the Platte River two years earlier. I hadn't seen her since Thanksgiving and, for the last month, hadn't returned her calls.

"What do you mean you *think* your hair is on fire?" The apartment my husband and I shared was near the L and the floor shuddered beneath me as a train passed.

"I can smell the smoke," she said.

"Do you see flames?"

"I can smell the smoke," she said again.

"Maybe you should call the fire department."

"I think I'll go outside for a while," she said, and hung up. I walked down the hall and sat in the linen closet.

I didn't tell my husband about the latest call. Just last week my mother had phoned to say my father had come home for breakfast, that his clothes were just a little wet and it looked like everything was going to be all right. But I did tell Dean, one of my summer school students. Since June, he'd been visiting my office every Thursday evening. He was a senior in college, an art history major; my etymology class was an elective he needed to graduate early. I'd been an assistant professor at the university for three years and always reminded Dean to ride the elevator to the eleventh floor, then take the back stairs down to my office on the seventh. I'll be up for tenure in a few years, I'd told him.

"Have you ever smelled burning hair?" I asked.

He shook his head. I was naked and sitting on my office floor, the blue-gray carpet rough against my legs.

"It's terrible," I said. "It smells like disease."

Dean was standing on the other side of the room, leaning against my desk, wearing only a pair of white tube socks. He had a swimmer's body, lean and broad-shouldered, though he tended to slump. Sometimes I pressed my palm against the small of his back to correct his posture. After I told him about my mother's call, he dropped his chin against his chest and sighed.

"It sounds like you should go back to Nebraska for a while," he said.

Since the drowning, I dreaded going home. In the nights before my last visit, I was kept awake by memories of traveling to Nebraska for my father's funeral, of the plane landing and looking out the window and seeing the Platte cutting across the state like a huge scar. My husband had come along, but spent the whole trip nagging me about visiting the cretaceous fossil exhibit at a nearby university museum.

"My mother's neighbors have been bringing her dinner every Sunday night for the last year, and she has a cousin nearby too," I said to Dean. "They'd tell me if something was really wrong."

"She doesn't scare you when she talks like that?"

"Of course," I said. "Of course she does."

It was then he walked across the room and held me, without desire, comforting me the way I imagined he might comfort his own mother. His skin was soft. He smelled like summer, like grass and sweat and white bar soap.

"It's time for you to go home," I said.

I found my husband lying on the living room floor, holding a photograph above his head. The sofa and glass-top coffee table were cluttered with newspaper pages, editorial cartoons from the *Chicago Tribune*, the science and technology sections from the *New York Times*. I asked if he'd remembered to buy more coffee filters and pick up my dry cleaning, and when he didn't answer, I nudged him with the toe of my pump.

"What are you doing?"

"Looking at a picture." He flipped the photo toward me. It was black and white. From where I stood, I could make out small, peaked waves.

"Is that a picture of Lake Michigan?"

"No," he said. "It's a picture of something *in* Lake Michigan." He sat up and pointed at a dark speck in the center of the photograph. "Right there. The monster is what I'm looking at."

My husband's career was going nowhere. In the spring, he'd left his job at the Lake Michigan Federation, where he'd been the assistant director of habitat management. After he'd been passed over for a promotion for the second time and dozens of academic presses rejected his book on the lifecycle of chinook salmon, he started spending weekends in his bathrobe and waking me in the middle of the night to discuss the injustices of academic publishing. He sent anonymous hate mail to the Federation and burned an issue of *The American Scientist* in the kitchen sink after reading an article about a PhD drop-out who had recently discovered, quite by accident, a new species of anemone.

Then one morning he got a call from the director of the Mishegenabeg Discovery Group, who wanted to offer him a position as expeditions manager, since he had extensive knowledge of Lake Michigan. Initially, he was skeptical of the group's practices, but came home from his first meeting impressed by their equipment and organization. And then, only a few weeks after joining the Discovery Group, he told me the mishegenabeg had come to him in a dream.

"I was underwater," he'd said. "Stuck there, but not exactly drowning, and I saw these huge eyes staring back at me. When I woke up, I thought about the sightings and disappearances that were reported to the Federation and how we always ignored them. I realized how wrong I've been."

"What kind of disappearances?" I'd asked, still thinking about the dream he had described, of being trapped underwater, but not drowning.

"How about the fishing tug that vanished near Port Washington a few years ago," he'd replied. "No distress call, no debris. Just gone."

"There are dozens of wrecked boats at the bottom of Lake Michigan," I'd said. "It probably just sank."

"Don't forget the scales the size of dinner plates that ichthyologist found floating in the lake last summer," he'd said. "They were never identified."

"Don't forget the size of some of the sturgeon and carp living in Michigan," I'd said. "You of all people should know."

"Laugh if you want, Diane, but I finally know what I'm looking for."

As an etymologist, I had tried to tell him the word "mishegenabeg" translated into "water snake," that whatever people had seen in the lake was probably just a big fucking snake, but he wouldn't listen.

From the floor, my husband reached for my hand. He had a bad back. I held his wrist and placed my other hand on his elbow. He pulled hard against me as he stood, his dark hair flattened to reveal the bald spot on the crown of his head. After the mishegenabeg dream, he threw out his bathrobe and started dressing well again, in pressed slacks and polo shirts. In exchange for his work with the Discovery Group, he was getting a small monthly stipend and had told me salaries and benefits were just things that kept us trapped in soul-killing jobs.

He tucked the photograph into a manila folder and placed it on the mantle, next to pictures of our wedding and a long-ago vacation to Mount St. Helens. He started in again on the sightings he'd heard about at the Federation, how most of them occurred late at night, how some said the creature was at least fifty feet long and the color of moss, how others described it as looking, from a distance, like an overturned boat floating in the water. He told me the Discovery Group had scheduled their first official expedition for September. They were trying to get a reporter from the Tribune to cover it.

"But you haven't been diving since college," I said. He'd gone to school in Maine and been a member of the college scuba diving team; during our courtship, I heard countless stories about traveling to the Gulf of Maine with the team on weekends to plunge into freezing waters.

"I was pretty good back then," he said. "Plus, Ada and Stephen have raised enough money to buy the group new regulators and air tanks."

"Who are Ada and Stephen?"

"Members of the Discovery Group," he said. "There are ten of us, which you would know if you took more of an interest. We already have three motorboats, and we're pooling money for new underwater cameras."

"So you're just planning to remain unemployed?" I pinched the bridge of my nose. At the Foundation, his salary had been comparable to mine and our rent had gone up a hundred dollars last year. "Perhaps it's time you started looking for a real job."

"Your hair seems different." My husband reached toward my head, then pulled his hand away, as though I might shock him. I realized I'd forgotten to brush my hair and sweep it back into the customary ponytail after leaving Dean.

"Don't change the subject," I said. "And don't think you're going to dip into our savings, either."

"What are we really saving that money for?"

"We could buy a house one day," I said. "We could travel more. We could spend next summer in the Yucatan."

"I'm going outside." Our little balcony had an iron railing, across which we'd strung white Christmas lights last December. After the holidays, I kept bugging him to take the lights down, finally giving up in March. He left the door open and gnats streamed into the living room. I was about to ask him to close the door when he shouted my name from the balcony.

"I forgot to tell you that your mother called," he said. "I took down a message."

In the kitchen, I found a note scrawled on the back of a grocery receipt: *not a fire, just smoke.*

All summer, I'd been trying to write a paper on the etymology of misunderstandings. I hadn't published much since my first two years at the university, when I placed three well-received papers with *Etymology Today*. Whenever the chair emphasized the importance of contributing to our fields at meetings, I felt her gaze falling on me. My background was in systematic comparisons, the study of what words had originated from their common ancestor language and which had been borrowed from other languages. What happened, I wanted to know, during the process of foreign words being adopted by another language—surely there must have been misunderstandings. At the start of the summer, I went to the department chair with my idea.

"Sounds more like theoretical linguistics to me," she said. "What happened to your paper on the etymology of corporate language?"

"It's going to take more time than I'd realized," I said. I had lost interest in the project months before.

"Too bad," she said, pushing a mess of brown ringlets from her forehead. "It's a timely subject."

That same afternoon, I went to see a professor in the history department and asked him to tell me about a significant misunderstanding between historical figures, thinking I could start by researching a story. I'm not interested in facts and hard data right now, I said, just talk to me. He looked up from a huge leather book with yellowing pages, told me a brief and unhelpful story about Napoleon, and then went back to reading.

One night in August, Dean wanted to watch the meteor shower he'd heard about on the radio. It was supposed to be the best one in years. He sat in the armchair behind my desk, naked save for the tube socks. He had once told me he wanted to be an architect, like Carlo Scarpa or Kevin Roche, and that he was already preparing applications for graduate school. I had taken this to mean he'd be moving away after graduating in December. In Dean's presence, I saw myself as I was in my twenties, the perfect, pale softness of my skin. But more than anything, I had come to appreciate how transparent he was, how easily understood: his excitement, his fear, his attraction, all put forth without reservation. I felt a jolt of relief whenever he talked about graduate school; he would leave on his own, I imagined, sparing me from having to become an instructor in suffering.

"When's it happening?" I was sitting in the chair across from him, still naked, my skirt suit a dark mound on the carpet.

"Tonight." He checked his watch. "In just a little while. We really should go see it." He stretched his arms over his head. "Have you heard any more from your mother?"

I told him that I'd given her neighbors a call and they'd said everything was fine.

"Still," he said. "You must be worried."

"*Meteor* comes from the Greek word *meteoros*," I said. "Do you know what that means?"

"Will this be on the next test?"

"It means *high in the air*." It had rained that afternoon, though the sky cleared at dusk. I picked up my red raincoat and wrapped it around me, tying the belt snugly at my waist. Dean rose and pulled on his shorts.

"So let's go up high in the air." I opened my window and pointed to the fire escape. Damp heat gusted into my office.

"Wouldn't that be dangerous?"

When Dean finished buttoning his shirt, I noticed he'd done it crooked. I walked over to him and redid the buttons, looking into his face, taking my time. "It's the only way to reach the roof," I said. "We have to get above some of the lights if we're going to see anything."

We climbed the side of the building like thieves. It was risky; security guards patrolled the campus at night and there was a chance we'd be spotted, but right then I didn't care. When we reached the top of the building, the winds were strong and my raincoat kept blowing open. My thighs hardened with goosebumps. I saw parking lots and a soccer field, the open wound of a construction site, a bright yellow pipe jutting from the hole like a robot's finger. In the far distance, Lake Michigan was black as a pit of tar.

"There's still too much light," I said. "We can barely see the stars." It dawned on me then that I should have been terrified. The fire escape was narrow and slick; I had no idea whether we'd be able to get down safely, and there was a chance I'd be caught with a student, at night, wearing nothing but a raincoat. I told myself that Dean would be moving on soon, that the end of summer was in sight, but none of those things explained the calm I felt on the roof, or why I was living as if these were the last months that would belong to me.

Dean glanced at his watch, the hands glowing neon green in the darkness. "It's almost time."

Seconds later, streaks of light moved behind the clouds, pale and swift as fish in a river. I tried to count them, but they were passing too quickly and I lost track after a few seconds. Something about all that light passing over my head, so far from my grasp, made my entire body throb. The four walls of my office felt very far away.

The next time my mother called, she asked if I'd seen my father. It was a few days after the meteor shower and my hands still ached from gripping the wet bars of the fire escape.

"Not in a long time." I had been the one to identify his body at the morgue after he was pulled from the river. I remembered the green bruise on his cheekbone, the bluish color of his skin, the way the veins in his face and hands resembled the intricate lines of a map. He'd looked like a Hollywood corpse, a dummy, a joke.

"He was here for breakfast and I haven't seen him since. Do you think I should start calling the neighbors?"

Her voice was calm. I pictured her standing on the linoleum floor of her kitchen, in a lavender housedress and slippers, bobby pins holding back her graying bangs.

"Dov'é," she said, Italian for *where are you?* The child of Italian immigrants, she had, in the last year, started speaking the language she'd abandoned as a girl. The L passed and I waited for the shaking to stop before I answered.

"Mom," I said. "Why don't I come to Nebraska next weekend, just to see how things are?"

"Oh, Diane," she said. "We don't live there anymore."

In bed that night, I didn't resist when my husband slid his hands underneath my nightgown. I didn't resist when he began moving over me in a halting rhythm. We hadn't made love in so long that his body had become unfamiliar to me. The broad hands, the dark circle of hair around his belly button. The lights were off. He could have been a stranger. He went soft before either of us could finish and lay on top of me for a minute, a big heap of man resting between my thighs.

After he rolled away, we were quiet for a while. He breath was deep and ragged, like someone trying to recover from a sprint. I stayed on my back, blinking at the darkness.

"Diane," he finally said, and when I didn't reply, he started telling me about his practice dives with the Discovery Group at Winthrop Harbor. He talked about how strange it felt to be sealed inside the rubbery wetsuit, how it took him a few tries to suck oxygen through the mouthpiece properly. When he first opened his eyes, it was the deepest dark he'd ever seen, darker than the waters of Maine, and he recalled a calming exercise he'd learned on the swim team, which was to visualize an empty white room.

"Do you realize how hard that is?" he asked. "To make yourself see only in white?"

"Haven't tried it lately." It was hot and through the open window, I heard traffic below, voices on the sidewalks. That afternoon, I'd left the university and gone to a nearby park, where I intended to think about my paper on misunderstandings, but instead I read a newspaper article on people who had changed their identities. A new social security number, driver's license, birth certificate, passport, name. It could all be bought. One person, quoted anonymously in the article, said he changed his identity every five years, so he never had to be the same person for too long. I watched teenagers kick around a soccer ball and wondered what I would choose for a new name: Betty, Raquel, Lucinda. I had planned to stay in the park for an hour and then return to school, but in the end, I didn't go back at all, even though I had student conferences. I called the department secretary and asked her to post a sign—*Out Sick*—on my office door.

"When I got to that place, to the white room, it felt like my head opened and my brain floated right out of my body," my husband said. "I was completely calm. I could have swum for hours."

I rested a hand on his stomach. His skin was damp with sweat. That evening, I'd found another message my husband had taken down for me on a paper napkin, this one from my mother's cousin, asking me to call.

"So let me get this straight," I said. "Your plan is to survey all three thousand miles of Lake Michigan with this group until someone sees the mishegenabeg?"

"We have to track it first," he said. "Pay attention to wave patterns and water levels. I am a trained scientist, in case you've forgotten."

"That's not the same as being some kind of explorer."

His stomach tightened underneath my hand. "People can change. What we want can change."

"I don't think that's true," I said. "I don't think we change very much at all."

"I've figured out what I want," he said. "Maybe you should do the same."

"I'm working on it." I pulled my hand away and shifted in the dark.

My husband turned on the bedside lamp and picked up *Mishegenabeg: The Myth of Lake Michigan* from the bedside table. "I'm learning the most fascinating things from this book," he said. The earliest sighting of the mishegenabeg had occurred in the eighteen hundreds, when the giant head of a snake emerged from the lake, dousing a boating crew in water. One crew member even claimed the monster had spoken to him in Latin.

"That's insane," I said. In the low light of the bedroom, my husband looked different; the stubble collecting on his cheeks and chin made his eyes appear darker, more remote. *What's happened to you?* I wanted to ask, and wondered if he would want to turn that question back onto me.

"Go to sleep, Diane," he said, opening the book. "And dream your dark dreams."

A different summer, five years earlier. My husband and I drove outside the city to see a botanical garden in Glencoe. We visited the bulb garden, where red and orange tulips were clustered around small stone statues of foxes, then the Japanese garden, which had raked gravel and gingko trees and water lilies. At the lakeside garden, we watched Canadian geese lumber from a pond, their bodies large and awkward on land, and looked for the birds listed in our guide—cardinals, egrets, warblers, wrens. We wandered the path that circled the perimeter of the property, passing a statue of Linnaeus and a little bronze bear and picnic tables stacked with flyers advertising a horticultural therapy program. We didn't follow the suggested route in our guide, but walked without direction, my husband occasionally reaching out and squeezing my fingers.

I could not say for sure that I was happier then, though when I look back on that afternoon, the bird-watching and the flowers, the day seemed to mark a turn in the path—as in, from there everything got worse. There was so much we didn't know in Glencoe: that my husband would be twice denied the promotion he'd been counting on and the book he spent his evenings and weekends researching would never find a publisher, that my father would have a heart attack while trout fishing and capsize his boat, that I would drop my dry-erase marker after seeing Dean in the back of my classroom for the first time. The truth was, in Glencoe my husband got impatient with me when I took too long exploring the bulb garden and, for a week after our visit, complained about the sunburn he'd gotten on his neck. The truth was, we got into a fight on the way back to the city, over an errant comment I'd made in the Japanese Garden, about how it depressed me to see so much beauty all at once, as though everything good in the world, or at least in Illinois, was contained right here. The truth was, that same week, in my office hours, I'd come close to taking a flirtatious student up on his offer to go out for a drink. The truth was, I'd always had recklessness in me. The truth was, things were already getting worse. But, in later years, I would not be able to resist re-writing that day in memory; I needed the altered version, I came to realize, in order to keep hoping for something better.

The last place we went was the waterfall garden, where a fifty-foot waterfall roared down a hillside and into landscaped pools. I was looking at a cluster of weeping conifers and rubbing the rough green leaves, even though the guidebook asked us to refrain from touching the plants, when I heard my husband, who was standing near the base of the waterfall, cry for help. I dropped the conifer leaf and rushed down the bank.

"What's wrong?" I asked.

"Nothing's wrong," he said.

"I thought you were calling for help."

"No," he said. "I was saying *heron, heron.* A black-crowned one just flew over the falls." He opened our guidebook and flipped through the pages. "It was really beautiful," he said. "I wanted you to see it."

On the hottest night in August, I had drinks with a friend who'd come into Chicago for the weekend. She used to be a university colleague, but had married two years earlier and moved to Aurora. At the bar, she ordered white wine. I ordered a whiskey, no ice. Right away, she asked about my husband. Her eyes were such a pale blue, I felt something inside me go cold if I looked at her for too long.

"How's he been since he left the Federation? Has he found something else yet?"

"In a way," I said. "He's still very interested in the lake." I wanted badly to tell her about Dean, about what we did in my office and going to the roof, about how it frightened me that I wasn't more frightened—for myself, for him. But I knew she would only lecture me about marriage and job security and good judgment. The life she was leading now would demand that of her. When she asked about my work, I told her I was making good progress on a new paper and expected to have a draft by the end of the summer. I considered the misunderstandings my imagination had started churning out during my office hours or when I was bored in department meetings: the rebellions that led to the Persian War started when Croesus misquoted the rate of tax increases in a proclamation; the Greco-Turkish conflict began over a misunderstanding about the borders of Crete.

"Did you know the War of the Pacific started over a miscommunication about using guano to make explosives?" I said.

"That's remarkable," my friend said. "Amazing, really."

I was preparing to spin her another story when she started telling me about something that had happened to her and her husband, Rick, earlier in the summer. "We went to Montrose Beach for the day," she said. "And this young man, he couldn't have been more than seventeen, swam out too far and got sucked into a strong current. Or so we thought."

The waiter came by and we ordered another round. My friend said the young man had been spotted by a lifeguard, but he was actually saved by someone who was already in the water—a woman who just happened to be a champion swimmer. My friend and her husband had watched the whole thing from the shore. They were there when the lifeguard blew his whistle, when the swimmer cut across the water, hooked her arm around the young man, and dragged him to dry land. My friend said it would have been a wonderful story—inspirational, even—if it weren't for the way the young man struggled against the champion swimmer, and when she finally yelled I'm saving you, I'm saving you, he cried back, I'd rather you didn't, I'd rather you didn't.

"He said it just like that," she told me. "'I'd rather you didn't,' I'd rather you didn't. Can you imagine?"

"Imagine working up the nerve to swim that far out, only to have your plans botched by some do-gooder Olympian," I said.

"I haven't been able to stop thinking about that day all summer," she said. "I couldn't tell you why. I know it affected Rick too. He refuses to talk about it."

My second whiskey was gone. I traced the edge of the glass with my fingertip.

"The boy was taken away by ambulance," she continued.

"He could be locked up in a hospital. Or he could have gone home and shot himself in the head." She stared into her empty wine glass, as though she might find something she'd misplaced there. "I wanted to find him and tell him I saw everything and that I hoped things got better for him, but Rick was against it."

"Maybe he made it," I said. "There's a chance he pulled through."

"I know this probably wasn't a story you wanted to hear, Diane." She wrapped her hands around the stem of her glass and leaned in close. "But it was just so troubling. I had to tell somebody."

"All bodies of water look the same to me now," I said. "Places to get lost in."

When the waiter came to see how we were, I asked for the check.

I knew my next meeting with Dean would be the last when he announced his plans to stay in Chicago after graduation. He sat on top of my desk, cross-legged, picking at the hem of his white tube socks. His pale shoulders gleamed. The young man my friend had told me about was still on my mind, and I wondered what it was—drugs? a love affair?—that made him swim out into the ocean and try to leave himself there.

"But the whole reason you wanted to graduate early was so you could go somewhere else," I said, getting dressed.

"I'd been thinking Columbia or Princeton, but DePaul or Loyola would be pretty good too," he said. "And then we could keep seeing each other."

"Dean," I said. "Where did the word marriage come from?"

"Latin. *Maritare*."

"And nightmare?"

"Old English. *Maere*."

"And story?"

"Latin. *Historia*."

"And trial by fire?"

"Old English, your favorite again. Comes from *ordal*, meaning a trial in which a person's guilt is determined by a hazardous physical test."

"Good," I said. "You're ready for the final exam."

"The final isn't for another week."

"Summer's almost gone," I said. "Time for the next thing."

"Why does there always have to be a next thing?"

"I blame the impermanence of existence."

"You think I'm so young," he said.

"You are so young."

"You think I don't have opinions of my own, but I do." He stood and stepped toward me, his arms outstretched. "I have lots of them."

"Dean," I said. "Put on your clothes."

"No," he said. "I won't do it."

His clothes were piled in a chair. I scooped them into my arms. I was tired of the games I'd been playing with him, of the games I'd been playing with everyone. I wanted to make sure he understood me. I told him it was fine if he wanted to be stubborn, that he could just spend the night in my office, then left. On my way home, I dumped his clothes into a trashcan. When I looked down, his jeans and boxers had disappeared underneath silver shopping bags from the Atrium Mall, but his black T-shirt was still visible, splayed across a red gasoline can. It would be a mistake, I knew, to keep looking at his shirt. To touch it. To smell it. I reached down and pinched the sleeve. For the first time, I noticed the collar was faded and pocked with tiny holes. I smelled gasoline, felt grease on my fingertips. I was tempted to take his shirt with me, a keepsake from the summer when I took my life apart, piece by piece, like someone unsolving a puzzle. But instead I just kept walking.

The next time I heard from my mother, her voice was a whisper on the other end of the line. Dean and I had been broken up for a week. He kept calling, first my office and then my apartment, and approached me in our last class, after I'd administered the final exam. He accused me of humiliating him; he said that if he hadn't dug through my office closet and found a commencement gown—which he wore home and didn't plan on returning—he didn't know what he would have done. He made a scene. The other students stared. When my mother called, it was the first time I'd answered the phone in days.

"Diane," my mother said. "I think your father is going to kill me."

"I don't think that's possible."

"He's been banging around in the basement all morning, making his plans," she said. "Last night, he kept shouting at me about the lawnmower. I really have no idea what's going on."

"That makes two of us." I walked down the hall and wedged myself into the cool dark space of the closet.

"I keep telling him that he should disappear," she said. "But he doesn't listen."

"You don't want to say that." I found my husband's baseball cap on the floor beside me and rubbed the brim, wondering how it had ended up in the closet, how *I* had ended up in the closet. "Mom," I said. "I don't know how much longer I'll be able to stay in Chicago."

"You could come here," she said. "You could help me with your father and the lawnmower and the doorbell."

"What's wrong with the doorbell?"

"It's broken."

"So where are you now?" I pushed the cap into the corner, underneath a stack of clean sheets. "If you're not in Nebraska."

"Da nessuna parte," she said.

The phrase she'd used this time translated into *get nowhere*. When I started to ask my mother what she meant exactly—as in, who was she getting nowhere with—she hung up. I stayed in the closet, holding the phone in my hands, feeling on the cusp of some kind of shattering.

Later that evening, I took a shot of scotch in the kitchen. My husband had started keeping his diving equipment in the guest bedroom and, even with the door closed, an earthy, raw smell had overtaken the apartment. I had another shot, then went to look at plane tickets online. I wondered what, when I got to Nebraska, I would say to my mother, if I would learn to comprehend the language she was now speaking, if I would know how to answer her back. I ended up studying the websites mentioned in the newspaper article on people who had changed identities: Metamorphosis, The New Life Institute, Disappearing Acts. They all looked like scams, all asked for money up front, and yet I couldn't help imagining myself as Betty or Raquel or Lucinda, couldn't help dreaming up a new life: I would go to some remote part of the West, near the Mojave Desert, say, and let my hair grow long. I would live in a trailer, so I could always pick up and go. I would write a futuristic account of a misunderstanding that led to a war that raged on for a thousand years, a war that could have been avoided entirely if someone had just said one thing differently. Finally I turned off the computer and stared at the dark screen. I wondered about the one thing I should have said differently, the one thing that set me on this irrevocable course.

That night I dreamed there was a heat wave so intense, the mayor ordered all the city's residents to take refuge in Lake Michigan. Soon the lake was packed with bodies. The water was hot. We bobbed there for weeks, all of us, even after our skin wrinkled and peeled. Then one day I looked across the lake, and everyone was gone except for some single, distant person—so far the face was a grey smudge. I felt something like relief, like recognition, and started to swim. Each time I thought I'd reached him, it was only a dark spot on the water.

I came home one evening to find the balcony door open and a strange noise coming from outside. Dean was still calling and my husband had been politely ignoring the phone calls I insisted go unanswered late at night. The department head had phoned earlier that day to schedule a private meeting with me. Her tone had been somber and clipped and after we set a time, she hung up without saying goodbye. I was in all kinds of trouble, and I knew it.

My husband was standing on the balcony, a tape recorder clenched in his hand. He'd turned on the Christmas lights; I noticed one of the bulbs had gone dead. I went outside and stood beside him. He clicked off the recorder.

"School's out," he said. "Any exceptional students this time around?"

I looked at him, startled, but he was already staring at his hands, not expecting an answer. I wondered if Dean or someone from the university had contacted him, or if he'd somehow known all along. I pressed myself against the railing, weak with terror and relief.

"I can apologize to you in fifteen different languages," I said. "Where should I start?"

"I'm not interested in the languages you speak anymore."

"Fair enough." I looked at my husband. The bones in his face seemed to be weighing down his skin. I asked what he had been listening to.

"An audio of the mishegenabeg," he said. "I got it at diving practice. A cryptozoologist in Wisconsin recorded it."

"Play it for me," I said.

A low, hollow noise surrounded us, like an echo bouncing around a cave. Or like whales conversing. Or a primordial groan. He played it again and again. Of course, the recording couldn't have been real, was something anyone with a little imagination could have made, but I didn't tell him that. I gazed at the lit windows staring back at us like eyes, at the glowing orbs of the streetlamps. This was the language he was trading in now, and I would have to adapt or not.

"What's going on with your mother?" he asked when the noise finally died.

"I don't know," I said. "I'm going to have to do something soon."

"And what is it you'll do?"

"I don't know that, either." I had so many ideas of what to do, ideas that felt at once intensely possible and as intangible as fog moving across Lake Michigan at sunrise. I could go to Nebraska and care for my mother. I could stay in Chicago and try to figure out how I had gotten to this point, surrounded by people I couldn't understand. I could finish my paper. I could write something new. I could help my husband search for the mishegenabeg. Or I could just disappear.

I looked out into the city, at the shadows between buildings, the peaks of skyscrapers. A row of people bicycling on the sidewalk below. A sombrero on a dumpster. The smog that sank against the tops of buildings like hair on a woman's shoulders.

"Look at that," my husband said, using the tape recorder to point out a distant building and the pair of lighted elevators rising and falling, so bright against the black of the structure.

"I want to be buried in a city," I said. "There's no such thing as night here."

"Lake Michigan's deepest point is nearly a thousand feet." He rested his arms on top of the railing and leaned against the iron bars. "It's so dark down there, nothing grows. It's called the hypolimnion layer."

I didn't say anything more. I watched the elevators rise and fall and thought about the people inside, imagining a group of four or six—couples, perhaps—gathered in one of the compartments, the slight rush of dizziness they would feel as the elevator ascended to the top of the building. Maybe they were laughing, or maybe they were completely silent. Maybe, just before the doors opened, they looked outside and glimpsed the white lights strung across our balcony, or maybe they didn't see anything at all.

still life with poppies

I.

In the spring, ivy grew over the only window in Juliana's classroom, the vines thick as a child's finger. During her last class, the afternoon sun fanned out behind the window and the leaves glowed a luminous green. After the students left, she rested her head on the desk. It was early May in Paris. Sunlight splashed across her arms and she felt heat seeping into her hands. The walls of her classroom were bare, the shelves unadorned with books or an aquarium filled with miniature turtles or jars of gray pebbles, like the mathematics teacher had across the hall. In fact, the only personal detail was the aluminum tin of dominos in her desk drawer. Sometimes, during her free period, she lined the dominos across her desk, seeing how long she could go before the rows tipped and the whole structure collapsed like a wave flattening on a beach.

She found a pack of Kleenex in her purse and wiped the sweat from her face, leaving dark smudges of mascara on the tissue, then unsuccessfully searched her drawers for a rubber band to pull back her long hair. She was expecting Mrs. Reinard, the mother of a student who had been doing poorly in her class, at any moment, and was surprised when the woman arrived thirty minutes late. She was dressed entirely in black, her dark hair coiled into a bun, her lips and fingernails painted red, a gold pin in the shape of a cicada fastened to the lapel of her suit jacket. She paused in the doorway before entering the classroom, framed by the fluorescent light of the hall, holding her purse against her stomach.

Juliana suddenly felt insecure about her French. She had been fluent for years, but retained an American accent.

She expected Mrs. Reinard's speech to be confident and throaty, a voice cured by cigarettes and good wine, but when she smiled and gestured toward the chair across from her desk, she strained to hear the whispered apology. As Mrs. Reinard took her seat, Juliana noticed a tiny run in the woman's stockings.

"I've asked you here to talk about your son," she said, folding her hands on top of the desk. "And his progress in my class."

"I gather he hasn't made much."

Juliana was aware some parents thought English shouldn't be offered in French schools, that it was an inferior language. As a result, several of her students didn't take her class seriously, submitted assignments late and didn't study for exams. She told Mrs. Reinard all this, then said what concerned her about Fredrick was not his performance in the classroom—he was, in fact, an average student—but the troubling behavior he'd started to display.

Mrs. Reinard adjusted her gold pin. "What kind of behavior?"

"Last week, a boy said something that upset Fredrick and he tried to stab him with his pencil." She didn't tell Mrs. Reinard that she hadn't been in the room when the incident occurred. One of the office assistants had called her into the hallway, and she'd told the children to review a chapter in their textbooks before rising slowly and walking outside, feeling light-headed, wondering if this had something to do with her husband, Cole, although it turned out the assistant just wanted to tell Juliana the afternoon teacher's meeting had been cancelled. When she returned to the classroom, Fredrick was sulking in a corner, the other boy crying and gripping the pointed end of a broken pencil. None of the other students would tell her exactly what had happened and she'd reported it as a minor scuffle. "Surely you received a call from the headmaster?"

Mrs. Reinard did not respond.

"I've also been finding these drawings underneath his desk." She opened a drawer and dropped a thin stack of paper in front of Mrs. Reinard. When she remained silent, Juliana added that she'd heard Fredrick had also attempted to smother the science class's pet frog.

Mrs. Reinard held up a particularly gruesome drawing: a man with red hair, his thin neck twisted as though it might be broken, plumes of blood shooting from his open mouth. The figure had no eyes or nose and appeared to be floating. It had the smudged, asymmetrical look of a Basquiat—but more lurid and frightening. "Fredrick drew this?"

Juliana nodded.

"The man is his father. I can tell by the hair." She pressed the sheet of paper face down against the table. "He left us in February," she continued. "Not a word. Just gone."

The first thing that entered Juliana's mind was, of course, her own husband, who'd disappeared in the fall, but she didn't mention that to Mrs. Reinard, nor did she say how Fredrick often looked at her during their lessons or when students were filing out of the classroom—a dead-eyed stare that made her stomach tighten, his green eyes unfeeling as stone.

"His father is fortunate to be on his own." Mrs. Reinard brushed lint off her jacket sleeve. "I really have no idea what we will do now."

Juliana suggested Fredrick start seeing the school counselor once a week, but Mrs. Reinard only shrugged and said she would look into it.

"Please do," Juliana replied. "It really might help."

"What about you?" she asked. "Do you have a husband with you in the city?"

"Not presently." Juliana glanced at the pale circle on her finger, a reminder of where her wedding ring had once been, a plain band with three rectangular diamonds. She had loved it at first, enjoyed the weight on her hand and the glint of the stones, but by their five-year anniversary, it had started giving her blisters and the diamonds had taken on a cloudy glare. The mark had started to fade during the spring. By mid-summer, she predicted it would be gone completely.

"How long do you plan to keep at this?" Mrs. Reinard flung her hand into the open space of the classroom.

"Perhaps through the fall," Juliana replied, even though she had not yet decided whether she would continue teaching English in the St. Germain district or return to the States or go someplace else entirely.

Mrs. Reinard rose and smoothed her skirt. "Paris is miserable in the summer."

"I'm not looking forward to it."

"You could travel."

"I could."

"Take my advice." She leaned across the desk and touched Juliana's wrist. Her skin smelled of gardenia. "And go to the sea."

Juliana was unable to find a seat on the metro—not surprising for a Friday evening. She stood in the center of the car, squished between two balding men and a woman cradling groceries. She peered into the paper bag and caught the scent of basil. Sparks of silver light flickered in the dark tunnel and she heard a whistling noise, as though they were burrowing deep into a cave.

Cole had never adjusted to Paris. He found the city crowded and dirty and, after being flashed by a man in a black trench coat on the metro, added perversity to his long list of complaints about the French. They had moved to Europe in August, when Cole—an economist—

accepted a two-year offer from the Bank of France and Juliana registered with a teaching abroad program. They had come from Boston, where she taught literature at a private school, and in some ways the new locale wasn't so different. She liked the city, the gardens, the cafés, the bridges, the craft stalls that lined the Seine. After the first few months, she even started dreaming in French: she was a hostess in a patisserie in one, a guide at the Louvre in another. But Paris also raised her husband's bothersome qualities to unbearable levels. He was irritable and narrow in his refusal to adopt French customs. She was always asking colleagues for restaurant recommendations and taking him places she thought he might like, but he was never satisfied. She fell into the routine of polishing off a bottle of wine every night just to quiet her nerves.

Still, the most startling changes in her husband didn't occur until the fall, when riots bloomed in a Paris neighborhood and spread all the way to the countryside. The violence was triggered by the deaths of two teenagers in the suburb of Clichy-sous-Bois. The boys, thinking they were being chased by police, dove over a wall and hid in a power substation, where they were electrocuted, their deaths unleashing waves of anger at the French authorities. In the months that followed, fleets of vehicles were burned, schools and public buildings destroyed, thousands arrested, power stations attacked. Before it was over, the rioters had spread all the way to Toulouse, Lille, Strasbourg, and Lyon.

It was a concern to her, of course. They had only been abroad for three months when unrest unfurled into chaos. Juliana checked the news each morning to stay informed and then went about her business: teaching, grading papers, buying baguettes and slabs of butter at the corner market, finishing the Balzac novel she'd been struggling through all summer, going to weekend art exhibitions and concerts.

She felt it was important to maintain her routines—just as she and everyone she knew had tried to do after the attacks in New York. But for her husband, it was not such a simple matter. He started leaving the office early to watch news reports, stepping out in the evening for a paper and coming home with four or five in his arms. And the cutting of the newspapers that came later: isolating articles about fires and assaults on police officers and spreading them across the kitchen table, as though they were puzzle pieces he was trying to fit together. Then, just after a state of emergency was declared in early November, he disappeared.

In the weeks before he vanished, Juliana found nests of paper scattered around the apartment. At first, the notes were connected to the riots: the times of special news programs, statistics on unemployment and poverty. But they quickly became more abstract, half-finished phrases and odd illustrations she assumed were economics equations: a shape that resembled a spider web with numbers and letters attached, intersecting lines and circles. Then one evening after work, she went for drinks with several colleagues, not bothering to call Cole and tell him she would be late. When she returned well past dinnertime, the door was unlocked and he wasn't in the apartment. She assumed he'd stepped out for a while, probably to gather more newspapers, and so she graded a batch of student exercises, relieved to have the study to herself, then went to bed.

When she woke at two in the morning and realized he still had not returned, something in her chest went slack. She stayed up the rest of the night, waiting in the living room in jeans and a pajama top, listening for the creak of the front door opening. He had been missing for three days when she came back from a meeting with the police and found a message on the answering machine. He had gotten out of the city and didn't want her to look for him. He said she would be getting some papers in the mail—

divorce papers, she thought at the time, although they never arrived—just before hanging up. Her sister, Louise, had been with her and re-played the message over and over. Even though they'd never been close, never shared the sisterly camaraderie Juliana envied in other women, Louise had insisted on flying from San Francisco to keep her company through the search.

"Do you really think that's his voice?" Louise had asked, after she finished listening to the message for the sixth time.

"Of course," Juliana had replied. "Who else could it be?"

"He sounds strange, doesn't he?"

"Wouldn't it be worse if he sounded totally normal?

Louise re-started the message. "What's that background noise? Is he in traffic? At a train station?" She bit her upper lip. "Maybe an airfield?"

When Juliana said she couldn't listen to the message anymore, they uncorked a bottle of wine and sat in the kitchen, where her sister eyed the answering machine as she talked about rising housing prices in California.

In the end, Juliana did not know whether he had gone back to the states or traveled elsewhere or remained in Paris. She had contacted his relatives and friends, searched all the places he frequented in the city, a wallet-sized picture in hand, called hotels and hospitals. He never returned to work, according to the Bank of France, and the police ended their investigation before the first snow fell. It could be a late-onset psychotic break, one officer had told her. Or perhaps some kind of mania. Her sister and the friends that visited—bringing along books on urban anxiety and personality disorders, things that were supposed to explain the turn her life had taken—had all come and gone by the end of spring.

Shortly after the metro had departed from the last station, the cars lurched to a stop, causing Juliana to stumble forward. The passengers muttered and swore and brushed against each other. It was incredibly hot, the air thick and sour. Juliana sipped her bottled water, then pressed the cool plastic against her forehead. The whistling was gone. The tunnel was quiet. She peeked into the woman's bag once more before the lights went out.

The passengers began speaking loudly, shouting complaints and questions. The car was still and dark. Someone pushed Juliana and she stumbled to the side, knocking into another person. She dropped the bottled water and it rolled across the floor. She heard something fall from the woman's grocery bag and splatter. Her leather satchel was heavy on her shoulder; she pulled it close. Something was swelling in her chest, hard and cold as Fredrick's stony gaze. In this black space, suspended beneath the pulse of the city, it seemed possible for all of them to disappear.

Juliana heard footsteps and doors slamming. The passengers quieted and migrated away from the center of the car. Three people burst into the space, carrying flashlights that omitted a dim glow. "Laiser passer! Police!" one of them shouted. For a moment, a flashlight shone on the leader and Juliana saw the dark blue uniform and the blunt nose of a gun. She was relieved until she realized they appeared to be chasing someone. Even after the officers left the car, the passengers remained silent. She wondered if some of them were remembering London, the images of smoke and crumpled bodies that had flashed across television screens. She couldn't stop thinking of Mrs. Reinard and her strange manner. Years from now, would the police find Fredrick clipping wires in a metro station or standing in a car with explosives belted around his waist? Was such a person here right now, a detonator hidden in his fist? It was then the lights returned and the train began to move.

The Hotel de Roch stood on Rue Chapon: a slender white building with a worn façade and a sign that extended into the street, flashing "hotel" in yellow letters. After Cole had been gone for a month and the police closed their investigation, Juliana moved out of the apartment. The two-bedroom was too large and expensive for her alone. She had spotted Hotel de Roch during an afternoon walk; it was only a few metro stops away from the school and guests were permitted to stay indefinitely. She had spent Christmas dragging luggage up the narrow staircase.

In her room, she switched on the small television that sat on the dresser and scanned news channels for a report on the incident in the metro, but found nothing. She went into the kitchenette and put a kettle on the stove, then sat at her desk and watched commercials for perfume and cleaning products before turning off the TV. She had scuffed hardwood floors that always felt cold in the morning and a single lamp on the bedside table, so there was never any good light. She had not unpacked her prints to hang on the walls and unopened cardboard boxes were still piled in a corner.

She heard footsteps in the hallway. The door opened and Leon stepped into her apartment. He had not shaved since she saw him earlier in the week and his white tee-shirt had specks of paint around the collar. He grew up on the southern coast of France—close to Spain, where he'd lived with his father after his mother died—and had maintained the room across the hall for two years. After a few chats in the hallway when she was still new to the building, he started dropping by on Friday nights for coffee. In the beginning, she thought it was possible something might happen between them, from the way he occasionally touched her knee, his eyes settling on her face with unbroken focus. But they had instead eased into something that was intimate and charged but managed to sidestep the erotic. When the heat was malfunctioning on their floor one evening in winter, they'd gone to Bistro d'Henri for drinks and she told him about coming to Paris and the riots and Cole leaving. I left all his clothes in the old apartment, on the bed, and my wedding ring on the dresser, she'd confessed near the end of her story, though she could not bring herself to tell him that she sometimes thought it would be easier if Cole had died, that she wanted so desperately to be done with the searching and the wondering that the certainty of death, of understanding what, exactly, she was mourning, would be a relief.

She waved Leon inside. "That is a look of desperation."

"What can I say?" He shrugged and rubbed the stubble on his chin. Like Juliana, he was in his forties. His eyebrows were full and streaked with gray, although his hair was still a rich black. He pulled up a chair and sat across from her. "The tourists aren't even giving me a second look. I need to have a new vision."

Leon split his time between waiting tables at a neighborhood café and standing outside the Pompidou Center in a skeleton costume. There were always a handful of street performers in the square; on the afternoons she had gone to see her neighbor, she counted a man who had painted his entire body gold, two violinists, and a teenager doing back flips. The head of Leon's costume was the most startling: five times the size of a human head with huge black sockets for eyes and jagged teeth. He alternated between jiggling his limbs whenever people walked by and breaking into a kind of grotesque dance, an open guitar case close to his feet. She took a photograph during her last visit: Leon leering at a pack of American teenagers, the shot mistimed so the skeleton head and the buildings in the background were blurred. She kept it on her dresser, propped against the side of the television. She thought of them as people between the acts, although he seemed to be handling limbo with more assurance.

The kettle whistled. She got up and made two instant coffees, knowing what he wanted—lots of cream, no sugar—without having to ask.

Leon sniffed his coffee. "This smells dreadful."

"I'm out of the regular," she said. "Don't drink it if you don't like it."

He shook his head and took a sip. She opened her purse and pulled out a sheet of white paper, a drawing she had found underneath Fredrick's desk this afternoon and chosen not to share with his mother. "Look at this." She handed it to Leon. "It's the worst yet."

Leon was quiet for a moment, holding the paper close to his face. The picture showed a man lying in what appeared to be a river, his stomach cut open and flushed with blood, the hands and feet missing. The man had the same red hair, like all the others. "A madman." He shook the paper. "I cannot believe he is only eleven."

"Today I found out the man in the pictures is his father."

"That's no surprise," he said. "Most boys hate their fathers."

When he gave it back to her, she folded it up and slipped it into a drawer, which contained several other drawings she had brought home, thinking it might be smart to collect evidence, in case something ever happened.

"Careful." Leon pointed at the drawer. "That stuff will get in your dreams."

"My dreams are already full of things I don't like," she said.

"Juliana." He finished his coffee and set his cup on the floor. "Would you consider going on a trip with me?"

This was not the first time he'd offered to show her the other regions of France, but she had always declined. The very prospect of travel made her tired and she was unsure of how to interpret the invitations, if he was making overtures.

"I work, remember?"

"We would leave tomorrow and be back by Sunday, traveling south." He stood and walked over to the photograph on her dresser. "It's supposed to be even hotter in the city this weekend."

She was already feeling worn down by the summer temperatures and imagined breezes gusting off the coastline. "What would be the purpose of our visit?"

"To go to the beaches. To get away from your students and those drawings and the heat. We'd take the train to Marseille and then drive to the coast."

"I'll think about it," she replied. "If I can have the window seat."

"Do you know how I got the idea for this?" He pointed at the photo. "When I was in Spain for the Day of the Dead celebration, I saw skeletons dancing everywhere."

"Sounds awful."

"At the time, it was a happy sight," he said. "But we've gotten off subject. Will you come?"

They agreed to meet at Café Concorde in the morning for coffee, then catch the nine o'clock TGV train at Gare de Lyon.

"I wouldn't drink another cup of yours if you paid me." He picked up his mug and put it in the sink.

She rose and kissed him on both cheeks. "So stop coming over for coffee."

After he left, she added her own mug to the sink and filled them with warm water. Then she opened her door and looked outside. The hallway was completely dark, the light by the stairs burned out. Things were always breaking down in the Hotel de Roch; her toilet overflowed three days after she moved in and the hot water once stopped working for an entire week. She went back inside and opened her window in time to hear a melodic siren passing on the street below.

II.

The morning train from Gare de Lyon was curiously empty for a weekend. Juliana leaned into the aisle to get a look at the other passengers, but could only see fingers and elbows and tufts of hair. She watched the blurred landscape, a swirl of yellows and greens with occasional bursts of red and violet. It felt strange sitting so close to Leon, their legs crowded together in the narrow space between the seats. She shifted and squirmed to prevent her knees from pressing against him, but after an uncomfortable period of keeping her legs pulled back, she relaxed and let them bump against his, a small gesture of intimacy that both comforted and unnerved her.

She told Leon about the dream she had last night. She was in the city, standing on a bridge that reached across the Seine, although she wasn't sure which one. The city was empty—somehow she knew this. The trees had lost their leaves and she could only hear the hollow sound of the river passing underneath. The gray buildings pressed against the sky like graves on a hilltop.

"Then my sister called and woke me. I couldn't go back to sleep or remember anything else." They flew by a cluster of stone houses, a dirt parking lot with a pair of dogs stretched out on their sides. "She always forgets the time difference."

When Leon asked why her sister had called, Juliana told him that Louise wanted to know if she'd given any more thought to her offer of the spare bedroom in her San Francisco loft. It seemed every friend or relative Juliana spoke with encouraged her to return to the States and resume her old teaching job or move to another city and start over, unable to understand why, after everything that had happened, she could stand to stay in Paris any longer.

"Have you given it any thought?" he asked.

"Not very much." It wasn't that she wanted so badly

to remain in Paris; more than anything, she was incapable of deciding, of striking in a different, unknown direction, and was frustrated by her inability to release herself from her life as easily as her husband had, a top spiraling across a flat surface.

"I visited her in San Francisco two years ago," she continued. "But I can't even remember what the city looks like now." When she thought of California, the only thing that came into her mind was the dense fog that hung over the bay, as though the clouds had sunk down to meet the earth.

The train entered a tunnel and the rush of darkness reminded her of the incident on the metro, which she relayed to Leon.

"I haven't seen a thing about it on the news," she said. "It was like we just fell out of the world for a moment, then jumped back in." She remembered the lights coming back on and seeing a shattered egg near her feet, the yellow yolk oozing onto the floor. "Toward the end, Cole became convinced the Metro was going to be bombed. By the time he left, he'd spent hundreds of Euros in taxi fares."

"I think your husband was afraid of the wrong things," Leon said.

"Really? Was he?" She crossed legs. "When I was down there, for a second I thought everything he'd feared was coming to pass. That he'd been in his right mind after all."

"But he was always looking to the outside, finding danger in shadows." Leon tapped his chest. "What about what's in here?"

Juliana suddenly felt restless and wanted to be off the train, in the open air. She asked Leon how much longer until they reached Marseille.

"Less than an hour," he said, pointing to the river they were passing. Juliana looked out the window in time to see the little blue and white boats tied to the banks, the paint gleaming in the sunlight, cheerful hostages.

After they arrived at the Marseille train station, she followed Leon into a parking lot, where he stopped in front of the Smart Car he'd rented and unlocked the doors. Near the end of the train ride, he'd mentioned wanting to drop in on a friend before going to the beach and she had agreed, wondering if they would be visiting someone from his youth.

Juliana sank into the passenger seat and opened her satchel to check her cell phone, noticing a new voicemail. When she listened to the message, no one spoke, although she thought she heard the faint static of breath, a low sound that deepened and shifted like wind. A wrong number, she told herself, although she couldn't help but imagine the caller might be Cole, phoning for something that couldn't be explained in a voicemail, and felt a flush spread down her neck when she realized the missed call was listed as an unknown number. Or, she wondered, could the caller be Fredrick. Her number was in the school directory, so it was possible. Was he angry that she'd spoken to his mother? What would he have said if she'd answered? It was too much for her, these pointless speculations. She turned off her phone and tossed her bag into the backseat.

"A good day for swimming," Leon said. He drove with one hand on the bottom of the steering wheel. The sun was full and shone brightly against his face. "After our visit, we'll go to the beach." He turned onto a two-lane road. "It's only a little farther south."

She hadn't been to a beach since her college years, always favoring the enclosure of cities. When the weather turned warm in Paris, she joined the groups who lay on the concrete banks of the Seine in their shorts and bathing suits or went to the enormous fountain near the Palais De Chaillot, where she could dangle her legs into the water and feel the spray from the fountainhead. She liked the anonymity of being deep in a crowd, of temporarily forgetting all the days that had come before. But a real beach, with pale sand and deep waters. She looked at Leon, cupping her hand over her eyes to block the sun. "I think that'll be nice," she said.

She leaned forward in her seat and watched the scenery, struck by the disparity of the terrain. She felt moisture in the air, yet the ground was dry and hard. One moment, the plants and trees were gray and arid, then they rounded a corner and were met with lush color. The land was flat for miles and then blossomed into impressive rises. They passed a vineyard, rows of low green plants, and an overgrown field with a dilapidated farmhouse in the center. In the distance, she saw the purple silhouettes of mountains.

She noticed a man walking down the road. He resembled, from afar, her husband, the same lanky build. He appeared to be wearing a pinstriped coat and carrying a briefcase, walking with a swiftness that seemed out of place in the country. But as they passed him, she realized his face, his soft features, looked nothing like Cole's; the briefcase was actually a toolbox, the man's jacket frayed and dusty. She recalled the early days of Cole's disappearance, scrambling to catch up to a man in the metro station, darting across the street to follow someone who had (she thought) his walk, staring through the window of a restaurant at a diner who held a spoon in the same way. She had grown used to these tricks of the mind.

Although they had lived on the outskirts of Boston and hadn't been directly impacted by the attacks in New York, Cole had fallen into a dark period that lasted until Christmas, attending every meeting on port and transit security that was open to the public and trying to push his way into some that weren't, detouring to avoid the busiest bridges, working from home as much as possible to limit his time in the Financial District. But it had passed and she never imagined a resurgence. After all, the media was flooded with stories about people suffering from post-traumatic stress; his behavior had seemed understandable. It wasn't until the Paris riots that she realized how much he'd changed, as though some dark seed buried inside him had found the ideal conditions for growth. And after he left, she was forced to recognize how she'd changed as well, her determined cheerfulness and willful ignorance, her ability to read the newspaper and then push the unpleasantness from her mind (how typical, how bourgeoisie, how very American, she thought now), as though the world wasn't shifting very much at all, as though everything wasn't disintegrating beneath them.

They passed an old couple standing in a pasture, rows of stone houses with pink and yellow shutters, and then a field of red poppies, the petals delicate and thin as tracing paper. She wondered if someone had planted them or if they had taken root naturally. She asked Leon to pull over and he did. She got out of the car and walked into the field. He rolled down the window and watched her.

She stepped carefully to avoid flattening the poppies. The soil was cracked and brown. It seemed miraculous that such brilliant color had emerged from this parched square of land. She bent over and pulled a flower from the ground. A breeze passed over the field, bending the stems of the plants. She crushed the petals in her fist, the little slivers of red pushing between her fingers like silk. The poppy was soft and damp in her hand. From the center of the field, it felt like she was surrounded by a thousand tiny faces.

"Hey," Leon shouted from the car. When she looked over, he was pantomiming a camera. He brought the imaginary camera to his face and made a clicking noise. "I'll call it still life with poppies."

She smiled and waved, then dropped the petals and wiped her palm on her jeans.

"You don't see flowers like this in the north," he said when she returned to the passenger seat. He started the car and pulled into the road. "Lavender," he added. "That's another thing that grows like wild over here."

"Question." She touched the red streak on her palm. "What do you think Fredrick is trying to say with his pictures?"

"That the world is too much for him." They turned onto a dirt road. White dust rose around the car. "Children say it all the time in different ways. The privilege is lost with age."

"If you were going to draw a self-portrait, what would it look like?"

He drummed his fingers against the steering wheel. "A bunch of lines maybe. Like a ball of string. Or maybe a big flat shadow."

"Do you remember the Henri Cross painting at the d'Orsay? The one that looks like it's made of a million little dots?"

He nodded.

"When I saw it, I felt like if I blew hard enough on the canvas, all those specks of paint would scatter." She tried to rub the red from her skin, but it barely lightened. "I would make something like that."

III.

They parked in front of a squat cobblestone house and got out of the car. Leon walked to the front door and knocked. An elderly woman answered. She was small, her skin freckled and creased. She wore a white linen dress with large pockets on the front and a black scarf wrapped around her head, revealing only a curve of silver along the hairline. Her eyes were small and dark.

The woman invited them inside, her French marked by an unfamiliar inflection. The house was small and low-lit. Juliana smelled rosemary and bread. The woman showed them to a rectangular wooden table, where she served herbal tea in clay mugs. The cups were shallow and Juliana finished her tea quickly.

"Leon," the woman said. "Are you still wearing the skeleton mask?"

"I haven't given it up yet."

"Keep going through the fall," she said, "And you will see something remarkable."

"The weather is very hot now," he replied. "The tourists stand around like dazed cattle. Few people give me money."

"Bear it," the woman said. Then she set aside her cup and smiled at Leon, showing crooked and stained teeth. He glanced at Juliana and nodded.

She produced three large stones from her pockets. They were inky and smooth, as though they had spent years in a riverbed. The woman made a triangular shape with the stones and covered them with her hands. Juliana nudged Leon underneath the table, but he just sat there with his arms crossed, staring at the woman and her bean-shaped stones.

The woman reached for Juliana's hand. She pressed her thumb against the red mark on her palm.

"From the poppies," Juliana explained.

The woman held onto her hand and began speaking in a dialect Juliana could not translate. She lowered her head and rounded her shoulders. Juliana felt heat entering her body; she imagined the woman peeling back her skin and studying the geography beneath. She did not pull away, too surprised for a struggle. When she asked Leon what was happening, he shook his head and brought a finger to his mouth. She was disturbed by her inability to comprehend the woman's language—I can't understand you, she wanted to shout—but the feeling of being shut out, of being unable to interpret, was also somehow familiar. The woman squeezed her hand harder, pressing the slender bones in her fingers together. She pursed her lips and hummed. It frightened Juliana to be dominated in this way, but a part of her wanted the woman to keep her pinned to the table, to dictate her next movement, and she felt a shiver of disappointment when her hand was finally released.

Juliana rested her elbows on the table and stared into her mug. She interlaced her fingers; her hands were hot and moist. The door was cracked open and warm air flowed into the house, the sunlight making a pattern on one end of the table that reminded her of Cole's equations, the bands of signs and symbols. After giving herself a moment to settle, she stood to leave and Leon placed a hand on her knee.

"Not yet," he said.

She returned to her chair. They sat in silence a little longer, then the woman reached into her pocket and gave Leon an old-fashioned iron key. He took it and thanked her. "Nothing is waiting," the woman said to Juliana in her accented French. She did not make any other gestures toward her before they left the house.

Juliana and Leon walked half a mile down the road and entered a garden. A low, rocky hill stood behind the foliage. They followed a gravel path, passing thickets of lavender and oleander before reaching a bench at the bottom of the hill. To the left, purple geraniums concealed their view of the road; on the other side, rows of Italian cypresses and sage-colored olive trees.

"Want to sit?" He pointed at the bench.

"All right." The wood was cool against her legs. Leon did not join her, instead standing in the shadow of a tree. "What language were you speaking back there?" she asked.

"A dialect from the Camargue region," he replied. "Where she's from."

She had read a little about Camargue, the marshes and pink flamingos and ranches that bred white horses. "Is that why we really came all the way out here?" She picked at the moss growing on the bench. "To see that woman?" She thought of how soothing the warm sand of a beach would feel right now, of leaning back and planting her elbows in the ground and looking out at an endless span of blue.

"That was one reason," he replied. "But there's something else."

She looked at him. "Well?"

He smiled. "Shall we go to the cave?"

She followed him to the hill, ducking underneath low-hanging branches. An arch had been carved into the rock, the entrance covered by a steel gate. Vines dangled in front of the bars like tentacles.

"The town installed this last year." He unlocked the gate with the key the woman had given him. "To protect the inside of the cave."

He stepped inside, leaving the gate open. Sunlight brightened the pale walls. The cave was much longer than it appeared from the outside. The light began to disappear as they went deeper and soon they were in total darkness.

"We're getting close now." A tiny beam appeared in his hand—a flashlight the size of a pen.

"How long have you known the woman we visited?"

"For years. My family vacationed in this part of France when I was a boy."

"Exactly what does she do?"

"She lives near the sea and goes to the garden. She collects those stones you saw and tells people about themselves. My mother used to visit her every summer, always on the first day of June, before she died. Her drowning was predicted one year before it happened." Leon stopped and faced the wall, then moved the light around. She was watching the beam slide across the stone when she saw a dark shape: a sketch of an animal, a horse or a cow.

"There." He pressed his hand against the wall. "This is what we've been looking for."

Soon the light revealed a black outline—yes, it was a horse—and three mountain peaks, the rock underneath shaded faint yellow and blue. The drawings were small, no larger than her fist. She stepped closer to the wall. "How old are these?"

"Thousands of years," he replied. "They were discovered by a group of geologists last spring. Scientists have come all the way to Marseille to study them. Another group is scheduled to return this summer. But my friend has a key. I don't know how she got it. She lets me use it whenever I like." He passed her the flashlight. "Here," he said. "See for yourself."

The coarse grain of the rock rose through the color, giving the drawings texture and ripeness. Occasionally the borders faded and it was difficult to tell where the shapes began and ended. She wondered what was supposed to be at the bottom of the mountains—a pool of water, perhaps. Was the dry land she had seen from the road once a sea? She heard Leon clear his throat and move away from the wall. She turned and aimed the light at him.

"What did the woman tell you?" she asked. "What did she say when she took my hand?"

"That she could see everything inside you," he said. "And then she told me what was there."

Juliana didn't press any further. She wasn't at all sure she wanted to know what was inside of her.

"You don't have to think about this now." He touched her elbow. "Just keep looking at the cave."

She pointed the light at the wall, the white circle falling on the horse. The neck was craned slightly and she could imagine the animal standing alone in a field, the intuitive angle of the head. She thought of the centuries that were contained here, the evidence of so many lives. She touched the stone and rubbed the damp grit between her fingertips.

For a moment, she returned to the apartment in Paris, to her husband standing in the kitchen, washed in the bluish light of evening. He was hunched over the sink, his hands gripping the edges of the counter. They had been arguing. She had been pushing him to get help and, in a flurry of desperation, even suggested they return to the States. She knew some kind of end was near. They had stumbled onto a path and moved too far, the ground now irretrievable. Sweat had bled though his white dress shirt, forming a pattern along his spine that resembled a ladder. He reached into his pocket and took out a ribbon of paper. Look at this, he told her, and tell me what it says to you. She had taken the note and stared at the jumble of numbers and told him it meant nothing. Nothing to her, nothing to anyone. Her marriage ending was not a shock; it was the spectacular strangeness of it that had left her staggering. She had been an ordinary person with an uneven marriage and a good job and the occasional adventure, unprepared for this life of peculiar and slippery grief.

The familiar weightiness came over her. She thought of finding Cole's notes, of holding the curls of paper in her hands and failing to interpret his secret language, and wondered if she was making the same mistake with Fredrick's drawings. Her husband and her student, it seemed, had been talking to her in the same way. It was something foreign and inaccessible and she wasn't at all sure she wanted to keep trying to listen.

Juliana heard footsteps and shone the light around the cave, but couldn't find Leon. She shouted into the tunnel, first in French and then, out of some hidden instinct, in her native language. The echoes stunned her—she couldn't recall ever really listening to the sound of her own voice. She took one last look at the drawings, then started toward the gate and the garden and the cobblestone house across the road. She pointed the light at the floor; the walls and ceiling went black. She kept going until sunlight spilled down the path and she saw the entrance. Leon stood underneath the arch, facing away from her, hands in his pockets. She stopped and turned off the flashlight. She wanted to know what the woman had said, every word, as though she needed to hear it aloud in order to set forth in a different direction. The sunlight was warm against her face and arms; dust had stuck to her skin. She held her poppy-stained hand like a wound, feeling at once dazed and urgent. She tasted salt and dirt in her mouth. Before she could call to him, he turned to her and asked if she understood what he had wanted her to see. "Oh, yes," she said, stepping toward the mouth of the cave.

what the world will look like
when all the water leaves us

Madagascar was not the first expedition on which I had accompanied my mother. We'd started traveling together the year I turned seventeen, after my father called from Alaska to say he wouldn't be returning from his ice-fishing trip and my mother, a biologist who specialized in rainforest primates, told me it was time I saw the world.

As we landed in Fort Dauphin, south of Madagascar's capital, the morning sun blazing copper through the small windows, my mother told me to stop calling her *Mother* and to start calling her *June*, adjusting her oversized black sunglasses as she explained *Mother* made her feel old and undesirable. In the year without my father, the same year she turned forty-five, her age had appeared on her face like a terrible secret. The delicate half-moons underneath her eyes hardened and crinkled, lines emerged on her forehead. Her hair grayed, though she'd dyed it blonde to cover the evidence. It was even startling to me, the person who saw her day after day. Sometimes I wondered if she wasn't in Madagascar to research deforestation and lemur populations for her latest book, but to charge through the vines and bushes in hope of finding some fountain of youth, to splash river water on her face and paste mud against her skin; to look for a cure.

My mother was a leading expert on primate habitats and a tenured professor at Cornell, although she'd been on sabbatical since my father left. Antananarivo University's biology department, concerned about the drop in lemur populations, was funding her Madagascar expedition. She had a theory that the lemurs, who consumed much of the fruit in the rainforests and buried the seeds after eating, were trying to re-plant their damaged habitats, but since lemur populations were lower in deforested areas, the rainforests would never regenerate without the lemurs there to plant the seeds. This theory, she had told me, would be the centerpiece of her next book.

After landing, we entered a black taxi and my mother directed the driver to Hotel Le Dauphin, where we would be staying for the next twelve weeks, on the island's eastern tip. *D'accord*, the driver answered. Nearly everyone in Madagascar spoke French, though my mother had taught me some basic Malagasy on the plane. Outside the airport, the taxi lurched down a pot-holed road, jostling us in the backseat. Such was the nature of travel in these remote corners, but my mother loved it all, the frantic car rides, getting off the plane and going right out onto the tarmac, the sky opening before her, dangerous and romantic.

By the time we embarked on the Madagascar trip, I'd been on sabbatical from high school for nearly a year and had given a lot of thought to what I wanted to do with my life. Somewhere between our first trip together—in the past year, we'd been all over South America and to New Guinea—and arriving in Madagascar, I'd decided to become a long-distance swimmer. I first saw the ocean in my tenth year, when I visited Montauk with my parents, who dressed me in flippers and goggles before sending me into the Atlantic. I remembered turning around, the water closing over my shoulders, and waving to my parents, their distant silhouettes blending together on the shore. It was the only time I recalled them standing so close. After Montauk, I started taking lessons at the YMCA and, in high school, joined the swimming team. By the time I started traveling with my mother, I'd accumulated a bedroom full of trophies.

I didn't see open water again until I spent a month in Uruguay, near the southern Atlantic. After my father announced his plans to stay in Alaska, my mother collected me from the high school I attended in upstate New York on a December afternoon, my hair still wet from swimming practice, and instructed me to pack a suitcase for Uruguay. Travel light, she'd said, and bring some bug spray. It was the first trip I took alone with my mother, who was there to study marmosets with a South American scientist named Alfonso. We stayed in a village inn outside the port city of Montevideo. I had my own room and only a few nights passed before I heard Alfonso's voice next door and my mother's laugh rising and falling like an echo. I spent my days on the village outskirts, staring at the marmosets she and Alfonso trapped in the rainforest for observation, small creatures that thrived on leaves and insects and had plumes of fur for tails. I ate eggs and sweetbreads and let the boy who sold empanadas slip his hands underneath my shirt. Some nights, I sat outside for hours and watched the river rush behind the inn.

During those days, there was so much I didn't know. I hadn't yet traveled to Argentina in a small airplane that shuddered as it swept over emerald-colored fields. Or returned to South America after only a few days of being back in upstate New York, of sleeping in my own bed and pocketing eyeliner from the neighborhood drugstore, because my mother's contact had called to tell her that after a logging company deforested a primate habitat, the marmosets started pushing each other from trees, and she wanted to see it for herself. I didn't yet know what it felt like to be too jet lagged to sleep or eat, to get bitten by a jumping viper and have a medicine woman suck the poison from my arm, to have boys throw empty beer cans at my bare legs because I was young and foreign and wouldn't let them lead me into a windowless room with a door that locked. Or to watch my mother disappear into the dark canopy of a rainforest and wonder if she would ever come back. Whenever I had confessed my worries, she told me that if you can keep brushing against death, little by little, fear will become a memory and you'll be able to face anything.

In the taxi, my mother pointed at a tall, crusty tree. "That's a triangulated palm. They're endangered, Celia, like everything else on this island." Then she described the lemurs I would see in the rainforests outside Fort Dupain: Black-and-Whites, Makis, Sifakas, Indris. "And in a few days, we'll meet Daud, a zoologist from Antananarivo University," she continued. "He's coming all the way from the capital to work with me."

The space inside the taxi felt too small, the air heavy and sour, so I rolled down the window. I was hanging my head outside, gulping down the breeze, when I heard the most terrible noise, shrill and gloomy, like an off-key trumpet. The sound came again and again, until I finally sank into the car and closed the window.

"That's the mating call of the Indri lemurs," my mother said. "Ancient tribes in Madagascar believed that if you listened to the Indris long enough, your body would turn to stone from the inside out."

I leaned back in my seat, wondering what my father would say if he could see me here. Things between my parents had been tense for years before he decided to stay in Alaska. Even with my door closed, I would hear them arguing about my mother's incessant traveling, "incessant" being a word my father used to describe many of the things she did.

An hour later, the taxi dropped us at Hotel Le Dauphin, a fancy name for a two-story stucco building the color of putty. Before I could unpack, my mother was at my door, ready to go exploring. We wandered through a market, the drumbeats and hissing fires drowning out the Indris, which had been even more audible from my hotel room. I asked about swimming, how far we were from water, but my mother wasn't paying attention. She ordered us red rice with grasshoppers from a food stand. No knives or forks were used in Madagascar, only large spoons. I started flicking the grasshoppers onto the ground with the lip of my spoon and my mother said, after all the traveling I'd done in the last year, that I should be more accepting of local customs, though I could tell she was dismayed by the food stand's use of paper plates. At home, she would, for conservation, wring the water from paper towels and hang them to dry. Once, when I had over friends from school, they made the mistake of commenting on the paper towels. My mother lectured them about the earth's dwindling reserves and, after dinner, she made us watch a documentary on the gibbons population in the Congo.

I poked the charred grasshoppers until they disappeared into the mound of red rice, then stared at my mother, trying to see her eyes through her sunglasses, a constant shield between herself and the world (she'd started wearing them all the time, even at night and indoors). We were physical opposites: my mother bronzy and tall, all sinew and bone, while I was dark-haired and small. It wasn't until I began eating that I realized the earth, the dust, was red too—deep and dark like an open wound. It had already stuck to the legs of my mother's jeans and stained the toes of my sneakers. I told her I couldn't eat any more rice, soothing her protests by remembering to call her *June*.

Daud arrived from the Capital on a Sunday. He was in his mid-thirties, handsome and broad-shouldered. When I first saw him, I was coming down the stairs. There was no running water that morning and I was going to see what could be done. Daud stood in the small space between the stairs and the hotel entrance. Many of the ceilings in

Madagascar had square holes that were only covered when it rained, and the sun beating through the skylight gave his skin a deep sheen. His nose was slightly crooked, as though it might have been broken once, and there was an unexpected delicacy to his ears. Their shape reminded me of seashells. A large patch from Antananarivo University was stitched onto his backpack. I stopped moving down the stairs. He turned towards me, his eyes narrowed in the light. I could hear the Indris; the heat was pressing against me. I had already gotten terrible sunburns, my shoulders flushed and peeling. My mother had joked that it looked like I was molting.

Before I could say anything, I saw my mother in the hotel entrance. If she noticed me standing at the top of the staircase, she didn't let me know it. She swept into the room, dressed in khaki pants and a loose white blouse and her sunglasses.

"I just watched two Sifaka lemurs nearly kill each other over a mate," she told Daud. "Don't they have an amazing way of fighting, the way they spin across the dirt like dancers?"

"Their kind of love makes ours look easy," he said.

"Did you know I was one of the first to photograph Golden-Crowned Sifakas?" my mother asked. "They were so rare, it took us weeks of trekking in the rainforest to find them. You've probably seen some of my footage." I watched her take Daud's arm and lead him outside, struck by how the light that made his skin glow only turned hers dull and gray. I knew she'd been rising before dawn to observe the lemurs—I'd often wake as she was bathing and dressing in the other room, as though our bodies were synchronized—and the malaria medicine had probably been giving her bad dreams. Her hair had looked brittle in that hotel lobby, her cheeks shadowed and sunken, although she'd also somehow never looked so beautiful, wearing her exhaustion with a regalness that seemed new to me. If I'd passed her quickly or been watching from another angle, if she'd turned her head towards the light a little more, I might have mistaken her for a stranger.

At the end of his days in the field, Daud returned to the hotel with red dirt streaked across his white T-shirt, usually humming a familiar-sounding song, which I eventually recognized as *The Impossible Dream*. He spoke English fluently, and I loved the way he could make my own language sound alluring. He told me about life in Antananarivo, teal and red motorbikes weaving around pedestrians, street vendors selling batik tunics and Zebu meat. About tribes in Madagascar that believed spirits dwelled in trees and planted one at each village entrance to keep away evil, about how the sprits abandoned the trees at nightfall and no one left their house after dark.

Daud spent his days with my mother, observing lemurs in the rainforest and trapping and tagging specimens, so they could analyze how deforestation had changed their patterns of eating and mating and nesting. Afterwards, we would have dinner together on the concrete terrace that extended out the back of the hotel. At these dinners, I became a kind of pet for my mother and Daud. During the day, they had lemurs in common and at night, they had me.

"Celia has the most astonishing memory," my mother said one evening, after we'd finished our bowls of lichee and mango. She asked me to recite one of the lists she'd taught me since my father left, like European cities with the highest crime rates or the most polluted places on earth.

"Come on," my mother urged. "Don't be modest. How about pollution this time?"

I would have preferred to list the names of everyone who'd swum the English Channel, like Lynne Cox, who'd done it when she was only fifteen, or talk about Lewis Gordon Pugh, who broke the record for the coldest long-distance swim in Antarctica.

"Ranipe, India," I began. "Then La Oroya, Peru, and Linfen, China." From there, I moved to Dzerzhinsk in Russia and Haina in the Dominican Republic and Kabwe in Zambia.

"And of course," I finished. "There's Chernobyl." My mother had always been fascinated by the ruined landscape of Chernobyl. Anyone who keeps a nuclear power plant in business, she liked to say, should have to eat their own plutonium.

"Peru?" Daud said in response to my list. "I wouldn't have guessed that."

"It's because of the metal processing plant in La Oroya," I replied. "And the toxic emissions of lead."

"What else have you got?" he asked, ladling lichee juice into his spoon.

"A list of all the famous scientists who've committed suicide," I said. "And how they did it."

"I didn't know that many had," he replied, then sat back in his chair and waved his hand, as if to say *but prove me wrong*.

I cited Adolphe d'Archiac, who threw himself into the Seine River, and Percy Williams Bridgman, who shot himself, and James Leonard Brierley Smith, who took cyanide, and Viktor Meyer, who also took cyanide. When my mother taught me this list, she said I needed to understand the toll answering important scientific questions could take on a person. After Viktor Meyer, I noticed Daud was staring at me, holding his spoon in midair, and I grew shy from his attention.

"Seems cyanide was the way to go," he said after I'd stopped talking.

"It does kill you pretty quickly," I said.

"June." He turned to my mother. "You certainly have given your daughter quite the education."

"Most parents shield their children from reality," she said. "But I wanted Celia to learn about hardship early on."

My mother started going on about pain being the root of knowledge, a Simone Weil quote she never attributed, but I had stopped listening. Instead, I looked at Daud, who was gazing at my mother, entranced, no doubt, by the way she spoke. The lilt in her voice still got my attention, even though I'd been hearing it all my life.

I kept in touch with my father after he settled in Alaska. He wrote me long letters about the endless dark of winter and the way the ice glowed silver during twilight and Lana, the woman who had been his ice-fishing guide. He was living in her cabin outside Fairbanks. I never told my mother how much I looked forward to his letters. Sometimes, if we'd been traveling for a few months, I'd find two or three waiting for me in New York. I was careful to not let her know when I started writing back.

My father was concerned that I wasn't going to school. I assured him that while I wasn't in the classroom, I was still getting an education of sorts. I had, for example, become fluent in Spanish and French and, in a letter sent from Hotel Le Dauphin, I wrote him some words in Malagasy—*Tsy azoko* for *I don't understand*, *veloma* for *goodbye*. I knew rainforests once covered fourteen percent of the earth, but now it was down to six. I could identify the medicinal sedges used to treat dysentery and fevers, explain how carnivorous plants digested insects. *As soon as she finishes her lemur research, I'll be studying right angles and Beowulf in New York again*, I kept promising my father in my letters, adding on more than one occasion that my mother had worked something out with my headmaster, which was a lie. I didn't know where my mother and I were headed after Madagascar, although I had a feeling it wasn't upstate New York. She'd always been a light traveler, but when she finished packing for this trip, her closet was nearly empty. Something had changed. I just didn't know what.

There were several times when I considered asking my father if I could live with him, but I never did—somehow sensing, without him ever saying as much, that Alaska wasn't an option for me. I did visit him once at Lana's cabin, three months before my mother and I left for Madagascar. Lana turned out to be a lanky, dark-haired woman, elegant in a quiet, vaguely sad sort of way. She had lived in Alaska all her life and had no desire to travel elsewhere. My father and I never talked about his leaving: we seemed to have a mutual understanding that what was in the past should stay there. He took me bird-watching every morning, and we observed great gray owls and American dippers through binoculars. In the afternoons, we went to a lake near Lana's cabin—a pond really, small and sunken and rimmed with brown grass—and listened to the arctic loons howl in the distance.

At night, Lana would fry fish and after dinner, we sat on the porch and drank beer until the stars pulsed. Our time together was pleasant, but cautious, like a trio of acquaintances leery of attempting more than small talk. One night, Lana told us the Inuits believed death dwelled in the sky and pointed out the aurora borealis, where you were supposed to see images of loved ones dancing in the next life. I searched for my mother, but didn't see anything that reminded me of her and was relieved. At the time, she was finishing a river expedition in the Amazon and if something had happened, I probably wouldn't have known about it yet. I stayed in Alaska for eight nights and during every one, I dreamt of Amazonian snakes: silvery blindsnakes and banded pipesakes, giant vipers and anacondas. I would wake in the early morning, kicking away the sheets in a panic, to make sure nothing was coiled at the bottom of the bed.

One evening, while my father and Lana were out on a walk, I searched a chest drawer for matches to light the kindling I'd arranged in the fireplace and found a bundle of letters. They were the letters I'd sent my father during my travels. As I unfolded them one by one, I was struck, despite less than a year having passed, by how young the handwriting looked: loopy letters that couldn't hold a straight line on the page. A child's handwriting, I'd thought when I finished reading them, the house dark and the fireplace still cold. A child's promises.

Every morning, my mother and Daud went into the field and didn't return until dusk. Once my mother, wanting me to do some exploring of my own, arranged for a villager to take me down the river in a *pirogue*, a canoe made from a hollowed log. At first, I thought the stretch of water that divided the rainforest might be a good place for practicing my butterfly, but every time I saw a crocodile basking on the banks, something in my chest clutched.

I tried passing the time by reading. It was cooler in my hotel room and I'd snuck some fashion magazines into my suitcase (my mother disapproved of magazines unless they had to do with science). After reading each one twice, I grew bored and moved onto the books my mother had packed for me, books about women having adventures: *Out of Africa*, *Jane Eyre*, *Delta of Venus*. But I couldn't concentrate with the Indris and the stories didn't really appeal to me, the mess of love and longing, women adrift. I would have preferred to read about swimming techniques, breathing control and resistance training. Some afternoons, I spent the whole day counting and re-counting the money I'd been hoarding since I began traveling with my mother: the pesos leftover from what she'd handed me to buy chajá cakes for her and Alfonso in Uruguay, the fifty-peso note she'd given me for a camera in Argentina, the stack of ariarys she'd allotted me when we arrived in Madagascar. Eventually I began leaving the hotel, but without the excitement I had earlier in the year, when life with my mother was still enticing. Instead there was a heaviness, a feeling of premature exhaustion and age.

I started taking long walks, stopping to examine pitcher plants and scorpions and huge Malagasy tombs—stone compounds decorated with bright geometric paintings and animal skulls. I said prayers outside the tombs, my folded hands smudged with red, and asked whoever was supposed to be listening to not let my organs morph into stone, for I kept dreaming everything inside me was oblong and gray. I took pictures until my film ran out. The last photo was of a passing bus. The hubcaps were dented and rusted, the windows rolled down. Everyone on the bus was singing. Sometimes, for no reason at all, I broke out running and keep going until my knees gave and I was gasping for air.

I found a little bar on the village outskirts, a dusty tin-roofed shack with wobbly chairs and an old radio that played dance music. On my first visit, the bartender filled my glass with a clear liquor that burned my throat. I returned every day for two weeks. I never saw another customer, but I didn't mind. I thought the solitude, the time away from the hotel, would help me sort out my life. I liked to think about what I would do once I returned to New York. Re-enroll in high school, get back on the swim team, practice with more dedication than anyone else. Sometimes I wondered what Daud would think if he saw me sitting in the bar, my sweat-soaked tank top clinging to my skin; I had seen the way my mother touched his forearm when she laughed, detected the smoothness in his voice when he called her *June*. One afternoon, after leaving the bar, I got dizzy and vomited on a plant with pointed leaves. I didn't go back again. During my time there, the only words the bartender and I ever exchanged were when I thanked him—*misaotra*—for the drinks.

It wasn't much longer before I heard Daud's voice in my mother's room for the first time. I listened carefully, but the sound of the Indris increased at night, and I just caught whispers and laughter and then Daud's humming. At dinner the next evening, my mother kept throwing significant glances in his direction, and he reached across the table to brush strands of hair from her face. It soon became their habit to only discuss fieldwork, rarely speaking to me directly. I sometimes caught my mother looking at Daud with a kind of possessiveness as she closed me out of conversations by talking science. I was left to drift in my imagination, to picture what my life would look like if I was away from here.

"Did you hear about the spider monkeys that attacked a tourist in Manja?" I asked them one night, just to see if I could get their attention. They had been talking about the nesting patterns of Pygmy Mouse lemurs for an hour. "I heard they scratched out an Italian woman's eye."

"Spider monkeys aren't naturally aggressive," Daud said. "They must have been provoked."

"And there aren't spider monkeys in Manja." For the first time that evening, my mother turned to me. "It seems your source was wrong, Celia."

She and Daud resumed their conversation about Pygmy Mouse lemurs. I went upstairs and took out the shoebox that held my money. I fanned the foreign bills across the floor and made uneven stacks with the coins. I spent the rest of the evening using my stash to create little towers and bridges and moats, a city of paper and metal, an escape.

My walks started getting longer, bringing me all the way to the coast. It took over an hour, but being near the water made me feel less restless. By the shoreline, the foliage was paler and drier, the hills lower, and then the landscape broadened into a wide curve of sand, speckled with gray rock and sea foam. I would wade up to my knees, nervous of going too far, of riptides and sharks. Each time, I promised myself I'd go far enough to feel the sandy floor disappear beneath me, the chill of deeper waters, but I never did. I was always looking for a point I could swim towards—a little clump of land or a large rock—but there was nothing: no land, just the sea, beaming like the sun had cracked open and seeped into the waves.

One afternoon, as I walked down the path that led to the sea, I heard a rumbling noise and turned to see a Jeep slowing beside me, Daud in the driver's seat, alone and waving. He offered me a ride. When I got in, I asked why he wasn't in the field with my mother, and he said they'd been working nonstop for weeks and he was taking a break.

"Thought I'd go for a drive," he said. "Maybe see the ocean."

"I go there all the time." I took my hair, stiff from sun and seawater, down and shook my head.

"Long walk," he said.

"It's worth it."

When we arrived, he parked on the edge of the beach. The ocean was blue and quiet. Daud removed his hiking boots, then peeled off his T-shirt and tossed it onto the hood of the jeep. I touched the point of his shoulder and, trying to channel the confidence of my mother's voice, asked if he wanted to swim with me.

"You should be careful," he said. "There are strong currents if you go out too far."

"It's not so bad," I said.

"Then you lead the way."

I jogged across the hot sand and into the ocean, hesitating when the water crossed my knees, but I heard Daud's footsteps behind me and kept going. After the water covered my shoulders, I swung my arms and kicked my legs, trying to look practiced and at ease. When I finally stilled, the muscles in my thighs quivering, I turned in the water. The coast was about half a mile away, shimmering like cut glass. Daud moved towards me in a leisurely freestyle.

"You've got good speed," Daud said when he reached me, his face wet and gleaming.

"I won three division swimming championships in high school." I thought of the trophies in my bedroom, the marble columns with little plastic swimmers affixed to the top. "I was runner-up in a state championship too. I would have gone to regionals if I hadn't left school to travel."

"Your mother must be proud," he said.

I looked across the water, not telling him my father was the only one who ever attended my meets or photographed me holding my trophies. I asked Daud about what surrounded Madagascar; he said the Mozambique Channel was six hundred miles to the west, the Mascarene Islands five hundred miles to the east.

"The record for long-distance swimming is just over two thousand miles, set by Martin Strel when he swam the

Mississippi," I said. "So it would be possible to swim the Mozambique Channel or reach the Mascarene Islands."

"Open water swimming is different," Daud said. "They're no lanes, no one to blow the whistle."

"I know." I pictured us going even farther, the low roar of the ocean filling my ears. "That's why I want it."

We didn't say anything more for a while. We bobbed in the water, the sun bright against our faces. The longer we stayed, the more distant the shore seemed. I found the openness both terrifying and intoxicating—a part of myself fighting the impulse to swim back to solid land, another part wanting to plunge myself into this kind of vastness again and again. I was afraid of so many things, I had come to realize during my traveling year. My mother seemed to have an immunity to fear, the way she hurled herself into foreign lands and the arms of men, while I was always entangled in ideas about penalties and peril.

I was about to ask Daud if we could swim farther when he disappeared, leaving only a blanket of ripples where his head had once been. I spun around, looking for him, waiting to feel his hands graze my knees. I stared across the water, one hand cupped over my eyes, and shouted his name. When he didn't surface, my body grew heavy with dread, with thoughts of sea creatures and underwater black holes. Then, without warning, he appeared in the distance, grinning and flapping his arms. Before I could call to him, he vanished again, this time staying under even longer, until I felt vibrations around my legs and he reappeared right in front of me, bursting through the water with the force of a sea god.

"How did you learn to do that?" I asked. "To hold your breath for so long?"

He told me that when he was young, he'd go swimming in the ocean with his brothers after school. "Some afternoons we'd race," he said. "You need to be strong. And to be able to hold your breath for a long time. We'd take turns pushing each other underwater."

"Can you show me?" I drifted closer to Daud, wondering if it was possible to cure someone of fear. "Teach me the way you learned?"

He rested his hands on my shoulders, our noses nearly touching. Water had beaded in his eyelashes, making them darker and longer. He stared at me for a long time. Then he thrust me underwater and held me there until I felt like my heart was going to explode. He released long enough for me to take a single breath, then pushed me down again. I opened my eyes the second time, saw dense shadows in the water and Daud's legs, and by the time he pulled me up, my lungs were aching. His hands slipped down my chest, his fingers momentarily clinging to my breasts, before he took me underwater again. Each time, he kept me there longer, his palms like stones against my shoulders. I twisted and squirmed, getting wild with panic, my fists thumping his chest and stomach. The last time he took me under, the back of my brain went fuzzy and I imagined death swooping down from the sky like a great black bird and just as a weightlessness started to wash over me, he let me rise for air.

"It's good for you to struggle against the water," he said when it was all over. We swam back to shore slowly, Daud's hand on the center of my back. "In case you ever get sucked down by a strong tide. You have to know how to fight."

When we reached land, I lay in the sand, exhausted. It was late in the afternoon. The sky was darkening. Daud sat next to me, asked if I was okay, and I nodded. My shorts and tank top were soaked, my white bra straps exposed. I looked down and saw the small ridges of my nipples. I didn't try to cover myself, feeling too tired and too brave. Daud's body was lean, his forearms and calves roped with muscle. He had a pale scar in the shape of a horseshoe on his chest. I wanted to press my hand over it, but sensed I should not. I told him about the lists I'd started keeping on my own, different from the ones my mother encouraged me to memorize. The one I thought about the most was famous disappearances: Amelia Earhart, Jimmy Hoffa, Ambrose Bierce. I wondered if the mysteries of their lives would ever be solved, how long someone would look for me before my name was added to such a list. He didn't ask me questions, just let me talk. We stayed there—close but never touching—until it was nearly dark.

We returned to the hotel an hour late for dinner. My mother was waiting for us on the terrace, her plate empty. As Daud and I took our seats, I noticed our plates were heaped with food. My hair, still wet, stuck to the back of my neck; my clothes were dusted in sand. Before I started eating, I tucked my bra straps back underneath my tank top. I was relieved Daud had put his shirt on before we arrived at the hotel.

"Turnips with garlic and ginger tonight," my mother said. "I'm sure it tasted better when it was hot."

"How did it go this afternoon?" Daud asked.

"I got amazing footage of the Red-Ruffed lemurs," my mother said. "When you see the clips, you'll wish you'd been there."

"It sounds like you managed well enough without me," he said.

"I always manage well on my own." My mother sat a little straighter in her chair before telling us meaningful scientific research was best done in solitude, that collective thought only diluted the strongest ideas. "Did Walter Buller have research teams?" she asked us. "Did William Swainson?

"June," Daud said. "They were working at the turn of the century."

"That's not the point," she said.

In the dusk, I couldn't see my mother's eyes through her sunglasses, though I suspected she was looking at me. I focused on scooping turnips with my spoon.

"Celia took me swimming today," Daud said. "I didn't realize she had such talent."

"You do have a few trophies at home, don't you?" My mother tapped her upper lip with her index finger for a moment, pretending to not remember.

She stood and dropped her napkin. "I already checked with the cook, and there's no dessert tonight." The sky was dark, the terrace lit only by the dim glow of lightbulbs hanging from a wire. She walked away from the hotel, towards the tall grass and trees. Daud looked at me, started to say something, then followed her.

I called my father once from Madagascar, a month into our stay. The hotel owner let me use the phone in his office. Lana answered and passed the phone to my father without saying anything. He asked after my mother and I told him that I didn't think she'd be returning to New York after all. I had been longing to tell someone about the way she was changing, how much she seemed to have aged in the last year and how hard she was pushing against it.

"She's not changing," my father said. "She's just laying her cards on the table."

"But why now?"

"Because she doesn't have to pretend she wants to live the same life that I do anymore."

"She's making me call her by her first name."

"When your mother turned thirty, she took off to Mexico for two weeks. She's never taken aging well," he said. "And I never understood why she was so interested in those lemurs. I always thought they looked like deformed cats."

"It's because they're starting to die. Too many trees are being cut down."

"It's just like your mother to pick something like that," he said. "It's not the lemurs she really cares about. It's being able to alter something bigger than she is."

"But couldn't she find another purpose? Something closer to home?"

"That's the problem," my father said. "She only has one. And it's not you or me, either."

I pressed the receiver against my forehead. Even in the hotel owner's office, the windows and door closed, I could still hear the Indris faintly. "I've decided to become a professional swimmer," I told my father.

"You mean like the competitions you did in high school?"

"Not exactly," I said. "I mean long-distance, open water."

"Why would you want to do that?"

"To go as far as I can."

"Celia," my father said. "Couldn't you pick something a little less dangerous?"

I wondered if he thought distance swimming was the kind of thing my mother would do, grueling and lawless. I told my father I had been swimming every day and was learning to not be afraid. I told him that I always imagined some world famous coach trailing me in a motorboat and shouting commands through a megaphone: *straighten your legs, keep breathing, reach like you're grabbing onto the person you love most.* I didn't tell him that when I was frightened by powerful tides or strange shadows, I thought of Daud holding me under, of the way he made me struggle, and kept swimming. Or that when I paused to catch my breath, I sometimes turned in the water and saw my parents on the shoreline, as I had as a child, two ghosts in my memory.

Not long after my swim with Daud, I heard shouting in my mother's room. It was late in the night. I had wrapped myself in a white sheet and was trying to read enough *Delta of Venus* to fall asleep. I pressed my ear against the wall, but I only caught foot-stomping and door-slamming, which made my room shudder.

It occurred to me then that I should go to my mother. When I opened the door, she was sitting on the edge of the bed, facing away, head in her hands. She was naked, her clothes heaped in the corner. Her sunglasses and the postcards she usually traveled with—pictures of the Andes Mountains and the Amazon River and the desert where the Aral Sea had once been—were scattered across the floor. Some of the cards had unfinished messages on the back, notes to friends and colleagues that were never sent. Her hair sat stiffly on her shoulders; her back was dotted with freckles. She'd lost weight since coming to Madagascar, and I could see her spine, curved and stretching her pale skin into translucence. She looked small and frightened, a huddled child. The sheets were tangled; the unshaded lightbulb hung from the ceiling at an odd angle. She was not crying, just sitting there, unmoving, and I did not know what to say. I closed the door, gently as possible, and went back to my room.

The next morning, my mother woke me early and said she was taking me to the rainforest. When I asked about Daud, she told me the lens on their spotting scope had cracked and he'd gone to a nearby village to have it repaired. We drove down a grooved dirt road for about a mile and parked in front of the rainforest's dense treeline, fat with spade-shaped leaves and vines. She sat in the driver's seat, pale and sweating, and I thought of the way her naked back had looked like it could have belonged to some primitive animal.

"Celia," she said. "Why have you been avoiding the forest?"

"I didn't know I had been."

"You're always thinking about water," she said. "We've been here for six weeks and you've never once asked to come into the field with me. Don't you care about what's happening to the lemurs? Don't you want to see them?"

"I hear enough of them." Closer to the rainforest, the Indris were louder than ever, cawing in a way that made me want to scratch my ears. "I really don't think I'd mind if they went extinct."

"Which would leave me with nothing," my mother said, getting out of the car. I sat in the passenger seat for a moment longer, waiting for the ache to fade, before joining her.

We carried backpacks; binoculars hung from my mother's neck. As we moved deeper into the forest, the light darkened. She was already a few feet ahead and I had to hurry to catch up. We walked an overgrown path, thick with tree roots, and while the Indris must have been unbearably loud by then, the noise was not what I remembered. I remembered walking behind my mother, the sweat seeping through the back of her T-shirt, the sway of her blonde ponytail. Her telling me about lemurs having symbiotic relationships with tiny birds and the five layers of the rainforest: the overstory, the canopy, the understory, the shrub layer, and the forest floor. She said each part had its own little ecosystem, its own little universe. And weren't people like that too, she continued, worlds unto their own. I began to wonder if I had been avoiding the rainforest after all, wanting so badly to carve out a purpose that I'd had to find my own landscape. Or maybe I had been frightened of what existed here, scared that whatever had intoxicated my mother would reach me too, that my own desires would disappear into the mist and heat and ceiling of green.

My mother stopped to peer at two ringtails through her binoculars. She told me it was unusual to see a pair, since they typically traveled in groups. I was glad we didn't spot any of the lemurs she and Daud had trapped and tagged. It pained me to imagine these ringtails being captured and sedated, my mother clipping little plastic bracelets around their spindly ankles and staring at them through the bars of a cage.

When my mother's right leg began cramping, we rested underneath a tree. I asked if she'd gotten leg cramps before and she nodded, adding that Daud got annoyed if she slowed them down. "Which is why you can't slow down," she said. "If you do, no one will wait for you."

"You've been working in jungles too long," I said. "People don't think like that everywhere."

"That's what you say now."

"Maybe we should go back to New York for a few months," I said. "I'd like to give school another try."

"You don't need high school," my mother said. "Algebra, sentence diagramming, spelling quizzes. None of that matters."

"You have a doctorate," I said. "You couldn't be here if it weren't for your education."

"Nothing I learned in the classroom is helping me."

"I miss our house." I picked up a handful of dirt, then let the black earth fall through my fingers.

"There's nothing for us in New York," my mother said.

"But what will you do?" I looked away when I realized I'd said *you* and not *we*.

"We should head back to South America," she said. Her sunglasses were crooked on her face. "More primate habitats are going to be deforested. A group of scientists are planning to protest outside logging companies, to stand in front of machines. We could be part of a resistance."

But what was there for me in South America? I wanted to ask. My mother must have seen something in my expression because she pointed out a Crested Ibis swooping between the trees. She always drew my attention to birds when she wanted to change the subject.

In thirty minutes, she was paler and sweatier and the cramp in her leg still hadn't passed.

"I think we should go back," I told her.

"I promised to get images of the Black-and-White lemurs today," she said. "They're at least a mile deeper into the forest."

So we got up and we walked. My mother didn't tell me the names of plants or tree frogs or anything else we passed. I knew she was unwell. She photographed the Black-and-Whites, who had a peculiar way of balancing atop bushes, and then we returned to the Jeep and drove to the hotel. Daud was still not back. In her room, she lay down on the bed without undressing. I took off my shoes and lay next to her. Open water swimming had changed my body; the muscles in my legs were harder, the skin on my stomach darker and tighter. I looked at my mother's arms. Her wrists seemed fragile, the points of her elbows too angular.

"Maybe I should call the hotel owner," I said, my voice nearly a whisper. "If you're not feeling well."

She shook her head, her sunglasses slipping down a little. "So you really want to be a swimmer?"

"I think so."

"When did this start?"

"While we've been traveling," I said, though I knew it had really begun long before.

"You have too much fear right now," she told me. "The man who took you canoeing said you wanted to turn back after passing the first crocodile." She rested her hands on her stomach. "When you commit yourself to swimming across a river or an ocean channel, you're committing yourself to the possibility of death. Your team, the people you train with, won't care if you drown or die of exhaustion. They'll only care if you break the record. And so that's all you can care about too."

"I've been practicing," I said.

"Do you swim until your legs are so tired that you can't kick anymore? Until you begin to sink?"

"No."

"See?" she said. "Still too much fear."

"That doesn't sound reasonable."

"Reason is overrated," she said. "Caution and beauty too."

We were quiet for a while, lying close enough for me to feel the heat of her skin, to smell the dirt and sweat. For a brief time, it was as calm as floating in a waveless body of water, someplace still and boundless.

"Celia," she finally said, her voice low and hoarse. "Do you think of me as *June*?"

"I've been calling you that, haven't I?"

"But in your mind. Am I *June* to you there?"

"Thinking of you as my mother is a pretty hard habit to break."

She sighed. And then she fell asleep. I stayed with her a little longer, staring at the cracks in the ceiling, spidery lines that reminded me of split earth. The room was hot. I was hearing the lemurs again, a blanket of noise like falling rain.

Daud returned late in the night and by the time I heard him climbing the stairs, my mother had been vomiting for hours. It had started soon after I returned to my room, when I heard retching through the walls and found her hunched over her small, rusted bathroom sink. Her sunglasses had fallen off and when she looked at me, I saw dark pockets underneath her eyes.

"Cholera," Daud said from the doorway. "She's been showing signs for a few days. Leg cramping, drowsiness. She's been filling her canteen with river water. I told her that wasn't a good idea, but she wouldn't listen."

"Why would you do that?" I shouted into the bathroom.

"I've been traveling for years and I've never been sick once." My mother was still leaning over the sink. "I'm supposed to be immune."

Daud said he needed to get an ORS packet, an electrolyte powder that would be mixed with boiling water. The cholera would pass in a few days, but in the meantime, dehydration was a danger.

"I have some packets in my room," Daud said. I noticed he was still standing in the doorway, that he hadn't gone to my mother.

While he was away, my mother became delirious. She said the lemurs were dead and the forests were burning, that a flood was going to sweep away the hotel and crocodiles would rule the island. The tops of her hands were beaded with sweat and I was almost afraid to touch her. I was relieved when Daud returned, carrying a canteen filled with a mixture of hot water and the ORS powder. He handed me the canteen and I kneeled on the bathroom floor and cupped the back of my mother's head in my hand. She drank without protest.

We moved her to the bed and I took off her shoes. I was surprised by the narrowness of her feet, the little clusters of blue and purple veins bunched on her skin like constellations. I smoothed her hair and noticed gray roots coming in, as though someone had painted the peak of her head with ash.

Just as I was drawing my hand away, my mother wrapped her long fingers around my wrist. "This is why I need you here," she said before turning from me and drifting off.

Daud and I went into the hallway and sat on the floor, next to each other, our backs against the wall. He gave me another ORS packet for the morning.

"I'm going back to Antananarivo," he said.

I asked Daud what my mother had done. Things hadn't ended well in South America when Alfonso saw her passport and discovered she'd shaved a decade off her age.

"Her theory is wrong," he said. "That's what we've been fighting about. Or that's part of it, anyway. Lemurs don't impact rainforest re-growth the way she thought. The deforested areas don't do better or worse without the lemurs and their seed-burying. The trees still start regenerating."

"Does she know she's wrong?"

"Knowing and believing are two different things."

"Maybe when she gets better, she'll come around."

"We both know that's not going to happen." Daud drummed his fingers against the scuffed floorboards. "Have you given any thought to getting out of here?"

"A little." I knew those moments of closeness, when we talked in the rainforest and in her room, when I poured the hydration mix into her sick body, would be forgotten once she'd recovered and was back to acting like all those human concerns, even love, didn't touch her.

"You could come back to Antananarivo with me. Stay in the city for a while, see if we can't find you someone to train with." Daud touched my elbow. His fingertips felt warm and smooth.

"I can't leave my mother like this," I told him.

Daud shrugged. "Would she stay for you?"

"I don't know," I said. "But I'm not her."

He rested his head against the wall, his throat curved and muscular, and started humming. I wondered what it would feel like to be in the company of a man who didn't know my mother, who saw me without the shadow of my origins. I would be free to offer a self I had selected and shaped, to pretend I knew nothing of science, that I'd never traveled beyond the New York state lines, that I only understood water and openness and quiet.

"You can't hear the Indris as much from here," I said. "If only I'd known that sooner. I might have slept in the hallway."

"The lemurs have gotten used to people over the years, gotten lazy," he said. "But some think they drove the first British colonists who attempted to settle the island mad." He told me the Latin root of *lemur* meant *ghost* because of the way they blended noiselessly into the rainforest and darted from tree to tree so swiftly, they were nearly invisible. He'd read travel journals from British sailors that described being awakened at night by screams, but never finding the culprits, and entering forests with the sensation of being followed, but never knowing what was tracking them, if something was there at all.

"Hard to believe they were actually feared," I said. "They just look like sad little monkeys now." I recalled the way some of them clung to the trunks and branches, as though their homes might topple at any moment.

"I wanted to give you these before I left." Daud took an envelope from his back pocket and handed it to me. "I shot them a few weeks ago."

I opened the envelope and found two pictures inside: one of an Indri, the creature that had been tormenting me so, crouched in the crook of a tree, timid and pitiful under the glare of Daud's camera. The other was of my mother kneeling on the rainforest floor, elbow-deep in black mud, as though she had hooked her fingers around a treasure and was dragging it to the surface.

Once my mother had fully recovered and Daud had been gone for a few days, I announced my plans to leave. I told her in the evening, while we had dinner on the patio. I had been swimming that afternoon—for the last time in those waters—and let myself bob in the sea like a buoy. My hair was still damp and smelled of brine.

"I'm tired," I said. "I need to go someplace familiar."

"You mean New York."

"I mean home."

"What will you do there?"

"Daud said your theory about the lemurs is wrong." We'd had a special dinner of curried fish, and I stared at the fine white bones on my plate. "What if he's right? Do you have other theories you could write about?"

"Important ideas are often discouraged by lesser people." She picked at her fingernails, which were rimmed with red dirt. She had started going back into the field, but still looked pale and tired. "You didn't answer my question."

"I'm going to swim," I said. "I'm going to find a trainer and practice and become great."

"You won't make it far, Celia." My mother straightened her sunglasses. "You don't have it in you."

"You have no idea what I have."

"Strangeness is everywhere and everything makes you tired in the end," she said. "When you figure this out, you'll be back."

I asked the hotel owner to arrange a taxi for the morning and then packed my bags. In my room, I counted my money, making sure I had enough for a car and a plane ticket. I planned to show up and wait until I could get a flight to the States, eventually ending up back in New York, where I would look for a job and an apartment near the Atlantic. I couldn't imagine ever making my way through the lanes of a swimming pool again; I had grown used to the expanse of the ocean, the sensation that I could, at any moment, vanish within it.

When I came out of my room the next day, I found one of my mother's postcards by the door. A desert was on the front and on the back she had written: *what the world will look like when all the water leaves us*, along with some statistics on the evaporation of the Aral Sea, formerly the world's fourth largest lake and once a popular training ground for distance swimmers. I tucked the card into the side pocket of my backpack, next to Daud's pictures. I did not know what my mother would do after Madagascar—travel to another foreign place and join a different research team or extend her stay in Fort Dauphin, though I was sure she wouldn't return to New York. She reminded me of a skydiver who'd cut the strings of her own parachute, volatile and doomed.

The taxi was waiting for me outside. The driver was a small man with a white beard. The top of his head barely reached the headrest. I was climbing into the backseat when I saw, in the far distance, a figure moving towards the rainforest. I asked the driver to wait and followed my mother down the road. I wanted a chance to say goodbye, to say the things we might not ever be able to say again. I stayed just close enough to keep her in sight. The sprawl of trees ahead looked bright and endless, an ocean of green. She had to know I was there, had to hear my feet tapping the red dirt, but she never turned around, never spoke a word.

When the driver honked, I stopped walking, as though I had been yanked by an invisible string. I watched until she became dark and slanted, imagining the cries of the Indris swelling, the vines bending underneath her boots; a moment that, over time, became like a scar on my brain—my mother moving down that crimson path, the ancient, knotted trees parting for her like a secret, the tall grass bowing like waves breaking on a beach, before her shadow disappeared into the sea.

acknowledgments

No [wo]man is an island, and so many people have contributed to the existence of these stories, in ways large and small. I am grateful to more people than I can include here; I hope you know who you are.

My gratitude to the editors who first supported these stories: Abdel Shakur, Tracy Truels, and Meghan Savage at *The Indiana Review*; Jill Myers and Stacey Swann at *American Short Fiction*; Susan Muaddi Darraj at *The Baltimore Review*; John Witte at *The Northwest Review*; the staff of *Third Coast*; Debra Liese at *The Literary Review*; Junot Díaz at the *Boston Review*; Hannah Tinti, Maribeth Batcha, and the rest of the amazing *One Story* staff; Elissa Bassist, Dave Eggers, and the *Best American Nonrequired Reading* selection committee; John Kulka, Natalie Danford, and Dani Shapiro of *Best New American Voices*; Bill Henderson of the *Pushcart Prize: Best of the Small Presses* series.

Thank you to the communities at Emerson College, Grub Street, *Redivider*, *Ploughshares*, *West Branch*, *Memorious*, and the Bread Loaf Writers' Conference. A special thank you to Michael Collier, Jennifer Grotz, and Noreen Cargill for the opportunity to learn so much and to make so many unforgettable friends. And a special shout-out to the back office crew: you are all rock stars.

Thank you to all my friends—most especially James Scott, Henry Cheek, Shannon Derby, Matt Salesses, Josh Weil, Benjamin Percy, Bret Anthony Johnston, and Robin Lippincott. You all mean the world to me.

Thank you to every teacher I've ever had, in particular Philip Deaver, for helping me get started, and Margot Livesey, for her brilliant instruction and unfailing generosity.

Thank you to Don Lee, for his wisdom and friendship.

Thank you to Connie May Fowler, for her sisterhood.

Thank you to Jacquie Berger, for helping me find my way.

Thank you to Katherine Fausset of Curtis Brown for believing in these stories and for being such a trusted advisor and dedicated advocate—the best any writer could hope for.

Thank you to Dan Wickett, Steven Gillis, Steven Seighman, Keith Taylor, and everyone else at Dzanc Books for their support, faith, and dedication. I will be in your debt always.

Thank you to my family, immediate and extended. My parents, for whom this book is dedicated. My siblings: Egerton, Gladys, Alexander, Alicia, David, and CJ.

My grandmother, Ethel Merritt, who offered solace when it was needed.

And finally, my deepest thanks to Paul Yoon, for being there.